JENIFER AND THE LOST

THE WIDOW'S BELL

The characters, names, and events as well as all places, incidents, organisation and dialogue in this novel are either the products of the writer's imagination or are used fictitiously.

For Mary, always better than I deserve.

For Sam whose courage and imagination started all of this.

For Ben for going out there and proving that it all actually *does* work!

One

To the boys of Millbrook Comprehensive Jenifer Andrews was all mixed-messages. Long, shining red hair, face of an angel and bright green eyes you could drown in, offset by a noisy, battered black electric wheelchair. A face to die for and a body that didn't work properly. To her few close friends she's Red, to the rest it was Dalek, Davros or worse. She didn't fit in either, no party girl this one; the school library had been gifted a hundred rare books a few years before. They sat neglected and unnoticed on the shelves gathering even more dust. Nobody ever looked at them, nobody except Red. She spent all of her free time in the library pouring over these unloved antiques, relics of another time and another way of life and few ever wondered why.

Red had two good friends, two real friends.

Eli, called Steve for short, was the strong silent type, he was also loyal and fair, fair minded to a fault. He'd fight the corner of anyone that was put upon. There wasn't a bully in the school that hadn't crossed swords with Steve and there wasn't a bully in the school that didn't regret doing so.

Then there was Jamel, known to everyone as Ethnic. He'd moved into the area from the Midlands with his family two years before. He found rural Monmouthshire a very different place to the streets of Birmingham where he'd grown up but he'd taken the move in his stride and settled in well. He'd made friends with Red and Steve on his first day and never looked back.

On one cold and foggy morning something really strange happened in the school. One of the gardeners, an eastern European guy that everybody knew (though none could remember his name) disappeared. He'd been at the school for six months, worked hard, always on time, always a smile never an argument. He was Polite and likeable, no problems or complaints from his bosses. So when one Monday morning he failed to turn up there was some surprise but that was nothing compared to the surprise of his body turning up three days later.

Another gardener was clearing a huge pile of leaves, sweeping them from the bases of the line of Elms that marked the western boundary of the school. Beneath the pile however, rather than playing field there was a pit. Five feet by four, straight edged, four foot deep and with the body of his colleague sat in the corner. The body had been completely drained of blood. He had a bite wound on his shoulder, chemical burns shaped like a child's hand on his forearm and the biggest smile you've ever seen on his face.

Attempts to keep the pupils (out on break when the body was discovered) from seeing what had happened, failed miserably. The initial surge, generated by the gardeners shriek on discovering his colleague, was soon replaced by pretty much all of the remaining pupils charging to the pit to see what had happened.

By the time the police arrived and with the teachers managed to gain some order and shepherd all of the youngsters back into the school. Several hundred mobile phones had photos of the unfortunate gardener and these had been shared and emailed long before the pupils were back in their seats.

Red had been one of the few unable to scramble to the edge of the pit but she was the first to get pictures emailed to her phone. Steve and Ethnic made sure that she could see what had happened.

As the crowd were steered back to the school, the row of excited chatter filled the air, everyone was surprised, everyone was amazed, everyone, except Red.

As well the police all over the school, the Headmaster Harold Williams also had to contend with a hastily planned combined visit from representatives of the local county council and the Welsh Assembly Government.

He was undaunted however, he'd been doing the job a long time and he knew what he was doing.

We join him as one of the senior police officers leave and a secretary brings the visitor from the council to his office.

'Mrs. James Mr. Williams' announced the secretary.
She showed the woman into his office where the two greeted each other warmly, they clearly knew each other well and were good friends. Harold asked the secretary to bring tea and pulled an unopened packet of Hobnobs from his desk draw.

'I leave you for a fortnight and the place turns into an episode of Midsomer murders! One of your gardeners?' Mrs. James asked still clearly surprised.

'Yes one of the ground staff, it's been an eventful morning.' Harold answered pulling off his glasses and wiping their lenses with a folded tissue.

'Did you know him well?' Mrs. James queried softly.

'Yes and liked him, been with us six months. No one had a bad word to say about him, not even Robbie and you know what he's like. Had to send his manager home she was in such a state.'

'Have the Police got any ideas?'

'Not saying, mind it's early yet. We've kept the school open they just cordoned off the area where he was found'. Harold replied thoughtfully as he slowly replaced his glasses.

Mrs. James nodded. 'Yes I saw the tent when we parked. She's gone to meet Jenifer in the Library by the way.'

'Yes I reminded her this morning. How are *you* finding Jenifer?'

'Positive, she's always so positive, we've recently got a newly diagnosed eighteen year old; she's got a progressive condition similar to Jenifer's. This one's not coping at all but Jenifer's emailed her a couple of times now and rung her, she's been a real help.'

The secretary brought in the tea as Mrs. James stifled a giggle.

'What?' Harold asked narrowing his eyes.

Between you and me, she asked if I could find out anything about your proposed Treasure hunt sanctions,' Mrs. James giggled causing Harold to laugh aloud.

The Headmaster had a thing about Treasure hunts; he had not one but two annual Treasure hunt events, held just before the main holidays and at Christmas. Pupils got themselves into groups of no more than six and competition was fierce. Jenifer and the boys had won the last four on the trot and the school social club talked openly of banning them the following summer.

'You're not going to allow them to be banned?'

'Of course not, problem is the three of them *are* pretty much unbeatable. The social club have said i've got to do something. I'll probably set them a few extra questions but even then they'll take some stopping.' He told her with a chuckle.

Harold spooned some sugar into his tea and stirred it as he

surveyed the goings on outside his window.

'It's more than just the treasure hunts though,' he began quietly. 'Any kind of puzzle or mystery and they'll crack it. You know those little cottages across the road from the back of the school?' (Mrs James nodded.)

'Well there's a Mrs Maybury in one of them, all the kids and teachers know her. Never anything out of the ordinary, she'd never done anything strange or odd. Then a couple of months back she's telling anyone who'd listen that there's a ghost in her house. She had the police round there, the council, even someone from the church. The house, attic and garden are all searched nobody finds anything, there's nobody in her house. General consensus was that Mrs Maybury was losing it.'

'But . . .?' Mrs. James asked.

Harold warmed to his tale, 'One of the girls in her year decided to volunteer Jenifer and the boys to solve the problem.' He said, smiling as he remembered.

Outside of a classroom a group of youngsters were waiting to go in, one of them (Jade) was talking to Red.

'I've told her you'll be round in lunch break with your losers.' Jade told her bossily.

Red was clearly not happy, 'Why didn't you check with me first?' she demanded.

Jade just shrugged, 'What else would you be doing?'

Steve and Ethnic were with Red standing beside her and in front of a long row of lockers.

Red turned to them as Jade sauntered into the class room. 'This is just typical of Jade she doesn't think. I'll never get into that cottage with this!' she told them thumping her chair.

Red's wheelchair was electric; she controlled it with a small joystick under her right hand. It was highly manoeuvrable but also large and heavy.

Steve and Ethnic both had their lockers open and were unloading books from their bags into their lockers.

'No worries, we'll grab a chair from the nurse's room. Need anything?' Steve said with a calm smile and a nod towards Red's locker.

'I've told you before, I never use it.' Red snapped back before adding 'Thanks' a little more gently.

The School nurse's room was a small cluttered untidy room with a few wheelchairs lined up in the corner.

There were two types of wheelchair and two of each. A Transit wheelchair had four small wheels and needed someone to push it. A Self-propelling wheelchair had two small front wheels and two large back wheels. The person in the chair could 'drive' this wheelchair by grabbing and turning the top of the large wheels.

'Good day or bad day?' Steve enquired.

On a 'good' day Red could manage a self-propelling but today wasn't a 'good' day (even without Jade's intervention).

Red nodded towards the transit wheelchairs.

'Would Madam prefer tatty black or nondescript grey?' Ethnic grinned.

'The grey one rattles.' Red moaned.

Both boys laughed, 'And yours doesn't?!' they echoed at last drawing a smile from their companion.

'C'mon let's do this' Ethnic enthused before adding, 'What can possibly go wrong?'
Red and Steve groaned in unison.

The cottages were across the road at the back of the school. The row of cottages was below and parallel to the road. Each cottage had a flight of concrete steps down from the pavement to their front door. The boys positioned themselves either-side of Red, now in the black transit wheelchair. Together they lifted the chair and started slowly and carefully down the steps, complaining as they went. Red gave back as good as she got.

'Stop squirming about!' Steve protested.

'You're tipping the chair!' Red told him.

'It's you moving woman, sit still!' Ethnic complained.

'How can I sit still when you're bouncing me all over the street?'

When they get to the front door they could see through the front window where a father and daughter (a toddler) were playing inside. Steve recognised the gun she was trying to 'shoot' him with. 'I bought one of those for my Nephew last week.'

'I think you've got the wrong house.' Ethnic told Red.

'I've got the wrong house?!'

Seeing them at the door the Father answered.

'Um hi, is this Mrs Maybury's house?' Red asked him hopefully.

'Sorry luv that's next door.' He jerked his thumb to the next cottage along. (This meant back up the steps and back down another set.)

The boys turned around carefully and started back up.

'Which part of sit still do you not understand?' Steve groaned.

'Look at the angle you've got me at, it's like sitting on a slide. Ethnic's got me a foot lower than you have.' Red protested.

'That's cos he's a foot taller than I am!'

Once they reached the next set of steps they found that their progress down was complicate by the presence of a handrail.

'You're right on the edge, move back in the seat.' Steve gasped trying to juggle Red and the handrail.

'I'm sliding forward because you're tipping me forward!'

'We're tipping you backwards cos you're leaning forwards!' Ethnic complained.

'You bounced me forwards when I tried to slide backwards.'

They finally reached the front door and rang the bell which was answered by a smiling elderly lady in a brightly coloured apron, she showed them in. Due to a step the boys needed to carry Red through the door and into a long and very narrow hall. With some difficulty they pushed and pulled her into a cheerful (but tiny) living room.

'Sorry about the step, I'll sit here cos I can't hear out of this one.' The lady told them pointing to her left ear.

She pulled a chair up opposite (and slightly right of) Red. The boys sat themselves in the two remaining chairs.

Red smiled at the slightly flustered lady, 'How long has this been happening Mrs Maybury?' She asked gently.

'It's Doreen darling and it's been a few weeks now, everyone thinks I'm going barmy. My daughters have been here, had their husbands over here. The neighbours have been over, the community support lady too; even the Vicar and I don't even go to church. But it never happens when anyone's here, it's only when I'm on my own.' She shook her head; this was clearly getting to her. 'I don't know what to do love, they've all searched the house, I'm here on my own, there's no one else here. But I hear him darling, I hear him, I'm not imagining it!'

She took a crumpled white tissue out of a pocket in her pinny and blew her nose loudly. 'I'm sure you've got enough problems of your own lovely.' She put her hand on Red's, 'I do so appreciate you trying to help but I don't know what you can do darling.'

Red's annoyance with Jade had evaporated now, one way or another they'd get to the bottom of this. As it turned out it wasn't going to take them very long.

'Tell me what the ghost says to you Doreen.' Red asked gently.

Doreen became upset, 'Oh it's horrible darling, that voice, that voice.'

'Take your time Doreen.'

'I'm here it says, I'll get 'er, then there's that terrible noise, like a fast clicking, cracking sort of a noise, then it says I'm coming for 'er, I'm coming, then he says I got 'er then there's the scream, a terrible, terrible high pitched scream.' Tears welled up in her eyes, she pulled her glasses off to dab her eyes with the tissue. 'There's someone in my house darling,

everyone says there isn't but there is.'
Steve and Ethic sat either side of Red quietly listening.
'Mrs Maybury is the clicking noise continuous or are there gaps.' Steve asked quietly.
Doreen gasped in surprise, 'Why there's gaps, yes there's gaps, why did . . . ?'
'Four clicks and a gap, four clicks and a gap.' Steve made a clicking noise with his tongue to demonstrate.
Doreen burst into tears and clapped her hands. 'That's it, you've heard it, oh you've heard it.' She leapt to her feet and grabbed Steve's arm. 'I knew it wasn't in my head, oh thank God and thank you young man, thank you so much.' Steve stood in an attempt to disentangle himself as she sobbed into his shirt.
Red and Ethnic stared at Steve in amazement, 'What?'
Steve made a gun shape with his hand and nodded at the far wall.
Red thought for a second, then grinned. 'Got it!'
Steve tried to peel Mrs Maybury off his shirt as Ethnic looked from Steve to Red still confused.
'It's the kid's gun next door but the houses are detached so you can't hear it, something must be picking up the sound.' Red whispered to him.
Ethnic stood up and surveyed the room; he soon spotted a small electronic device next to the phone. It was plugged in but switched off.
'Mrs Maybury what's that?' he asked pointing to the device.
She climbed out of Steve's shirt and looked to see what he was pointing at.
'Oh that's my alarm love if I have a fall I can press this.' She

had what looked like a plastic key ring with a button on it, on a cord round her neck. 'If I press this they talk to me on that,' she nodded at the device.

'But if you fall in another room?' Red queried.

'That's how it works love, if I press this accidentally, they ask if I'm okay and I can answer. If there's no answer then they know something's wrong and they'll send an ambulance.'

'Why's it switched off Mrs Maybury?' Ethnic asked.

'Oh it's knackered darling,' she told him.' I dropped the teapot on it when the 'Strictly' final was on. Still works but buzzes something terrible. I can't hear the buzzing what with my ear but it drives me visitors mad. So I switch it off when I've got guests.'

Red and the boys smiled. 'Pop next door and ask him if he's got an electronic baby alarm, if he has, ask him to switch it on and say hello. 'Red whispered to Steve.

Steve left the room as Ethnic checked the cable on the device. 'Flex is okay so it must be the unit,' He announced.

'Doreen I think we might have found your Ghost, would you mind switching your alarm on.' Red asked.

Mrs Maybury did so and sat expectantly watching Red and Ethnic as the device buzzed annoyingly in the corner.

'That lad knows about the clicking, he's a nice lad, strong silent type isn't he?' she said after a moment.

'He has Aspergers.' Red and Ethnic answered together.

Doreen pulled a face. 'Ooh poor lad, I've heard of that.' She sympathised, 'I've got some really good cream in the bathroom, does wonders for my feet, do you think it'll help with his rash?'

Before Red or Ethnic could correct her a loud clicking wail filled the room causing Doreen to leap to her feet. 'That's it, that's it' she shrieked pointing to the ceiling. 'He's here, he's here!

Steve's voice rumbled out of the device, twisted and distorted, sounding like something out of Night of the living Dead. 'This is Steve calling are you hearing me?

'It was him that nice young man it was him?' Doreen slumped back down in her chair looking astounded.

Back in his office the headmaster finished his tale, 'Pretty soon it was all cleared up.' He paused to liberate a chocolate Hobnob from its packaging. 'The little girl's plastic gun had been bought from Raglan Post Office, the same place that Eli had bought one for his Nephew. When you pulled the trigger, a plastic wheel with four raised lugs, span on the back of the gun. These lugs struck a lug inside the gun as it span over it. The noise produced was like a clicking machine gun, the harder you squeezed the trigger the louder and faster it became.' He dunked the Hobnob and took a bite. 'The dad had a game with the little girl where he'd crawl around the living room chasing her, whilst she 'shot' him with the gun then when he caught her she'd scream with delight. They had a radio baby alarm in the house. This was always switched on when she was put to bed. If she wasn't tired he'd play the game with her and if they were near the alarm this would be picked up. Mrs Maybury had a radio receiver in her alarm which was obviously tuned to a similar frequency. This alarm picked up the sound signal transmitted by the baby alarm in the house next door.

Because it was damaged it distorted the sound by greatly magnifying the bass and because Mrs Maybury could only hear out of one ear, she couldn't work out where the sound was coming from.'

Mrs James grinned, 'Fantastic' she laughed taking another Hobnob herself.

'They solved it because they thought to ask what the ghost was saying rather than just going in there to prove there wasn't anyone else in the house.' Harold finished.

'I am indeed impressed!' she told him reaching for her teacup.

Harold offered her another Hobnob. 'Oh there's more, wait til you hear what they did next.'

Harold sat back taking full advantage of his expensive padded leather revolving chair. 'During assembly one morning Janet a local PCSO had told the pupils that a pensioner had gone missing the day before.' He told her brandishing his Hobnob. 'Janet knew that there would be several groups out running because the school was in the build up to the cross country running competition with Monmouth comp. So she asked them all to be on the lookout for him. Now Jenifer knew the PCSO and wanted to help but obviously she wouldn't be going out on a run. She caught up with Janet after the assembly and got some more details. The man called Bert Evans a WW2 veteran had Dementia but it was in the early stages. As a sergeant pilot he'd flown Fairey Battles in 1939 and 40 but had been invalided out of the RAF following a bad crash. He was on a reunion coach trip; they'd stopped at a pub near to the school and then continued. Over the course of the journey Bert had been sat in two different seats talking to different groups on the bus. When the bus continued on its journey from the pub, each group assumed that Bert was with the other so nobody noticed that he hadn't got back on the bus. The alarm was only raised three hours later. The police searched the nearby town and garden centre as well as the school but there was no sign of him.'

Harold paused to bang on his window and point at a third year who'd been taking photos of two police officers struggling into crime scene coverall's outside the tent covering the crime scene.

As the youngster beat a hasty retreat, Harold resumed his tale.'

Jenifer wanted to help but didn't know how to. Then over the course of the morning lessons she started to realise that she might be able to help after all. She knew the pub and remembered the view from the back of the pub well. This was the only way somebody in a wheelchair could enter as there were steep steps at the front. The toilets were at the back of the pub.'

'She knew the pub? - are anymore of your sixteen year olds experts on the local hostelries? 'Mrs. James scolded with a twinkle in her eyes.

Harold laughed, 'Hardly, she meets up with her sister there first Thursday of the month, sandwiches and a coke. Now may I continue?'

Mrs. James smiled and nodded, enjoying his story as much as he was enjoying telling it.

'Anyone looking out from the back of the pub would see miles of rolling Monmouthshire countryside and in the distance just one building in the middle of a large open field. The building was used for farm storage; it was a long semi circular building very much in the style of an old RAF Nissan hut.'

'Jenifer reasoned that an old airman in the early stages of Dementia, perhaps a little confused, is out with former colleagues for the first time in years. They're all talking about the war, sharing stories and remembering. A couple of pints, he goes to the loo then when he comes out he sees the hut across the field. What if he wanders over, there's nothing to stop him but that shed is much further away than it looks. Once she'd got the idea she couldn't shake it, come lunchtime she sought out the boys and told them. They all knew about Dementia, as they'd all had it in their families or known somebody affected by it.'

'Yes her Granddad I remember,' Mrs. James nodded.

'The hut was a five minute drive from the school,' Harold continued. 'They were soon on their way.' He remembered.

There was a parking bay near a gate that opened into the field. Steve and Ethnic soon had Red out of the car and they could all see the hut some distance away in the middle of the field. There was no path so both boys grabbed a side of the chair and set off across the bumpy ploughed ground carrying their friend.

'It's like being on a boat, can you not keep the thing level for like half a moment?' Red moaned frantically gripping the chairs arm-rests.

'People pay to go on boats.' Steve replied unimpressed.

'If you'd sit still we'd keep you level.' Ethnic pointed out.

'I can't sit still cos you're bouncing me all over the field!' Red protested.

'How long's half a moment?' Steve asked.

'Yeah a moment's non-specific, how can it be half . . . ?' Ethnic started.

'I'm getting sea sick, people pay to go on a cruise, calm steady luxury, with you two it's Pirates of the bloody Caribbean!'

'People pay to see Pirates of the Caribbean!' Steve said.

The building itself was on a large concrete hard-standing, although tufts of grass and some Buddleia were pushing up through the many cracks in it. It was solid and level enough for Red's chair. The low winter sun was shining brightly but it was still bitterly cold as they made their way along the one

side and round to the door on the front of the building.
It was locked, Steve shook it hard but it was secure. 'Well he didn't spend the night in there.' Steve said with some relief.
'Bert' Red shouted as the three of them turned slowly around looking at the neighbouring fields.
'Have a try Ethnic,' Steve suggested knowing that Ethnic specialised in loud.
'Sergeant pilot Evans.' Ethnic screamed. A startled Magpie climbed into the sky but nothing else moved and it was eerily quiet.
'If he'd have come this way, there'd be nowhere else to go.' Red said glumly, then added more cheerfully, 'Looks like I got this one wrong let's get back to lunch break.'
They turned and started to head back along the other side of the hut. This side was darker and there was still frost on the ground glistening in the buildings shadow. There was frost on the grass as well as on the concrete and it even covered a little pile of sacking on the floor in the corner, except -
'Oh God,' Red gasped as she looked at the sacking, 'is that a shoe?'

The little frost covered pile of sacking did indeed have a shoe sticking out of it. The three of them hesitated before slowly and gingerly edging toward it.

Sergeant pilot Bert Evans, wartime Battle pilot, husband, father and grandfather, lay where he fell. Curled into a ball, he'd rolled down his sleeves and pulled the collar of his shirt up as high as he could. There were a few discarded filthy sacks on the ground, he'd tried to pull these over himself as a makeshift blanket but he hadn't had a chance.

'Oh look he hadn't even got a coat.' Red whispered her eyes filling with tears.

The three of them stood there silently, it was the saddest thing that they'd ever seen.

'You got to say something for him red.' Steve said quietly.

The three of them bowed their heads as Red mumbled a prayer.

Steve took his blazer off and placed it carefully over Bert's face. Ethnic rang the police and an ambulance but they all knew that Bert was past any help that could be given.

Back in his office Harold paused to release a further Hobnob from its packaging. 'The police and an ambulance arrived together; the ambulance crew were with Bert in seconds but soon confirmed that nothing could be done. Bert was put on a stretcher and carried with as much dignity as could be managed to the ambulance. A WPC followed Jenifer and the boys back to the school and took a statement from them in my office.'

'That is remarkable!' Mrs James said shaking her head.

'Made the paper!' Harold pulled a newspaper from a tray of files on his desk. 'The Raglan Press got hold of the story. Their editor had had a run in with the local police and he used the story to get his own back. Here see for yourself.' He

passed the paper to her.
A photograph of the school dominated the front page, the headline '**School children solve case that police couldn't**' blazed above it. The attached article referred to the local police with words like hopeless and clueless.
'A follow up article titled 'Police fail war hero' did nothing to soothe relations further and although none of this had originated from Jenifer and the boys, the local bobbies are still a little touchy about the subject.' Harold added.

In a corridor behind Harold's office Red was discovering just how true her headmaster's words were as she slowly rattled along the corridor. She'd searched for Janet the PCSO but there's no sign. So with some trepidation she approached a young and very tall fair-haired officer stood outside Chemistry one. He was flicking through his notebook.
'Hi, I'm . . .' she started.
'I know who you are.' The policeman replied coldly.
'I was wondering . . .' Red continued undeterred.
'If we need your help? - No miss you see we're professionals. He raised his head to look down at her. I'll warn you not to go meddling this time miss.' He snorted.
'Look that article wasn't our fault; we had nothing to do with it.' Red tried politely.
The policeman raised his eyebrows then turned on his heel. 'Don't interfere miss, we know what we're doing.'
Red sat quietly for a moment, clearly frustrated maybe Steve and Ethnic had done better.
Steve appeared looking equally frustrated.
'And . . .?' Red asked without optimism.

'I got nowhere fast, Ethnic's gone to use his natural charm and charisma on the little WPC on the gate.'
Ethnic appeared a moment later.
'Natural charm and charisma aye? How did that work out for you?' Red asked.
Ethnic was suddenly interested in his shoes. 'Erm . . . well um she's a bit of a strange girl that one. 'He mumbled.
'Okay so we've all struck out but we've all got a free afternoon. Anyone fancy a trip to Aber?' Red asked stoically.
Steve wasn't impressed. 'Trumps being inaugurated today, the world will probably end tomorrow and your choice for our last afternoon on earth is Abergavenny?'
'I need more information and the Library there has one of the books.'
Steve and Ethnic looked at each other decidedly unconvinced.
'I'll buy you both a coke.' Red said with her sweetest smile.
Steve and Ethnic grinned and nodded.
'When?' Steve asked.
'I've got *Ms* Clarissa Carrington-Smythe in the library first.' Red told them.
'With the lead piping?' Steve quipped.
Red grimaced, 'She's with the government or something, says she won't keep me long.'

Back in his office Mr Williams and Mrs James were still working their way through their tea and hobnobs.
'So county combining visits with Welsh Assembly now, what's this Ms Carrington-Smythe like?' he asked.

'Just joined apparently, straight out of uni, got a two one, very smart, very ambitious and *very* politically correct.'

The headmaster froze, dunked hobnob halfway between cup and mouth.

'Politically correct?' he asked looking horrified.

'Oh definitely yes, very much so!'

The end fell off the Headmasters Hobnob and splashed down into his tea. 'Oh dear!' He said quietly.

Red and the boys entered the Library; they found Ms Carrington-Smythe perched on a desk at the far end of the room.

She was young (not looking much older than Red) she wore a jarringly pink suit, with a pale blue shirt and pink tie. Her short blonde hair and makeup were immaculate. A huge bunch of keys beside her on the desk were attached to a fob with the logo Disco queen (also pink) and her handbag bore the logo Disco chic. As Red got closer she noticed in particular her shoes and nails both of which must have cost a fortune.

The boys headed for the other side of the Library.

'Hello Jenifer, super to meet you.' Clarissa gave her a huge cheesy smile.

As Red reached her Clarissa remained perched on the desk (and looking down at Red).

'Yeah Hi.' Red couldn't take her eyes off the woman's nails.

'Jenifer i'm spearheading an Assembly Government full inclusion initiative," Clarissa began.

'Do tell.'

'It's called positive thought breeds positive outcomes.'

'There's nice!'

'We're going to teach you how to unlock within yourself the power of a positive mental attitude.' Clarissa continued breezily.

Red could see where this was going. 'Oh right – I see you're saying that disability can be overcome with . . .'

'Stop right there - we don't use that word anymore!' Clarissa interrupted pointing a glossy pink pencil at Red.

Red wasn't impressed, 'What word?'

'Disability that word is full of negative implications. We prefer mobility impediment' she answered waving her pencil as if she was waving the word away.

'Impediment!' Red bit back.

Steve and Ethnic had tried to stay at the back of the library, keeping their heads down. But they knew Red well enough to see what was coming so started to edge towards her.

Red eased her chair towards Clarissa and leaned forward in it to get as close as possible to the girl.

'Yes Jenifer an impediment is something that might, if you allow it . . .' Clarissa started to explain speaking very slowly and deliberately as if she was trying to explain a words meaning to a child.

Steve covered his eyes with his hand whilst Ethnic slowly shook his head, open mouthed.

Red started slowly, 'An impediment is a cold, a cough, the

flu. An upset stomach, a headache, a dodgy curry last night. A trip or fall, a bad day at work, traffic on the way home; it's no change for the bus, not enough sleep, cramp on the sports field. An impediment is something that might get in the way, might put you off your stride now and again, maybe slow you down for a while.'

'I am not able to walk or to run, to jump, or to swim, to climb trees, or roll in the grass. I can't chase boys, or be chased by boys. I can't stand in the shower, nor try on a dress in a shop, can't stand and talk or stand and stare. I can't explore the countryside, I can't play Basketball, or soccer, or Tennis or squash. I can't get upstairs, I can't get downstairs. I am not able to dance Ms Clarissa Carrington-Smythe; I am not able to dance with my friends.'

Steve and Ethnic were clearly uncomfortable, despite the banter, they both cared about her. They were stood beside her now, not saying anything but in there with her.

Red continued, 'my life is waiting in the surgery, waiting in clinics, waiting in the hospitals. My life is new treatments, or there's *no* treatment. Conditions, complications, side effects, unforeseen side effects. Drug trials, new drugs, old drugs, mixed drugs, tablets, pills and injections. Waiting, hoping, trying and struggling Ms Carrington-Smythe. Always struggling! Struggling with zips, struggling with clasps, struggling with clips, struggling with clothes, struggling with keys, struggling with opening things, struggling with closing them, struggling with . . . ' She stopped, breathing in deeply, torn between crying and hitting the woman.

'I am Disabled Ms Clarissa Carrington-Smythe in that I am not *able* to do the things that I want to. I am not *able* to live the life I would choose for myself and that won't change because some manicured bimbo plays with a dictionary.'

Clarissa stared back at her open mouthed, 'I that is - the government are merely trying to create a positive mindset in those . . .' she flustered.

'You don't promote positivity by belittling the problem. Who are you to tell me how I should think or act? How can you understand me? How can you begin to put yourself in my position when you're starting point is to deny the position that I'm in?'

Clarissa stared blankly back, mouth in gear but brain in neutral.

'I think you've said enough now!' Steve told Clarissa.

'I'm inclined to agree,' the headmaster's voice boomed from the back of the library.

Harold Williams Headmaster was in the room, nobody had seen or heard him enter but everyone knew that he was there now.

'If you'd come with me Miss Smythe, *now* please.' He told her firmly.

Clarissa Carrington-Smythe her face nearly as red as her

lipstick shuffled out of the library like a prisoner walking to the gallows.

Ethnic shook his head, 'How does he do that?'

To the pupils of Millbrook Comprehensive their headmaster possessed an awesome supernatural power. He had the ability to appear whenever anything was going on. If a fight started behind the canteen he'd be there. If you took your girlfriend to the hidden spot round the trees at the back, he'd be there before you arrived. If ever anything happened at the school that wasn't supposed to, he'd be there. One of the prefects said after the gardener was found, the most surprising thing about it all was that when they found the body, Williams wasn't down there in the pit with him.

'You okay?' Steve asked Red.

'I'm always okay, take me to Aber.'

Two

Abergavenny Library was a small but impressive stone building on Baker Street, 5 minutes from the Castle street car park.

There were two steps up to a narrow door but Steve and Ethnic were easily able to bundle Red through without too much difficulty and head for the desk.

A pretty but tired looking blonde raised her eyes from her computer screen and smiled at them. 'Hi can I help?'

'Yes, we're from Millbrook comp. we need to look at Argonath four please, It's for a project.' Red answered.

The librarian frowned and prodded her keyboard. 'It's out I think, let me check, yep, i'm sorry it's out on an indefinite loan.'

'Indefinite loan, what's that?' Red asked confused.

'It means that one of our members particularly wanted this book. The book hadn't been out at all, so they made a donation and we allowed them to have the book for an indefinite period. We don't normally do this sort of thing but what with all the cutbacks . . .' the librarian replied looking genuinely sorry.

'Indefinite period?'

'They're not keeping the book, look I can arrange with them to bring the book back here on a convenient day for you, if you like.' She smiled reassuringly.

'Can you tell us who's got the book?' Steve asked.
'I'm afraid I can't tell you that.' She answered politely.
Red turned her chair around and Ethnic and Steve bent into a huddle.
'We don't have time for this.' Red whispered.
'The information's still on her computer screen Steve's got his phone; we just need a diversion Red.' Ethnic whispered back.
Red turned back to the Librarian. 'Okay then no problem, can you give me your card and I'll ring you when we get back to class and I can check our timetables . . . to . . . to' Red paused and placed her hand across her eyes, 'Oh.'
'Jenifer are you okay?' Steve asked sounding worried.
'Jenifer?' Ethnic echoed equally concerned.
'Tablets, I need . . . tablet' Red moaned.
'Tablets yes, tablets, heck where are they?' Ethnic replied panicking.
'Back . . . in the Back – 'Red gasped.
'Back of what.'
The Librarian leant over her counter pointing to Red's backpack on the back of the wheelchair (this was in effect her handbag as it was always on the back of whichever chair she was using.)'Backpack I think she means the backpack, the tablets must be in there.' She shouted.
'Of course, the backpack!' Ethnic pulled a zip back on the top pocket of the backpack; he struggled to pull a small

round silver tin out of the pocket. The librarian seeing him struggle leant over to try and help. Abruptly the tin popped out, bounced on the wooden counter top (knocking the lid off) and then onto the floor.

The bright yellow 'tablets' went flying in every direction, with surprising athleticism the young librarian vaulted over her counter and joined Ethnic (both on their knees) grabbing the 'tablets' which were rolling across the floor.

Whilst this was going on Steve, still stood by the counter, leisurely pulled his camera phone out of his pocket and leant over the counter to hold it out in front of the Librarian's computer screen. He took a few pictures, which he checked before pocketing the phone and joining Ethnic and the Librarian on the floor.

As the Librarian started putting all the tablets back in the tin, Ethnic took one and popped it into Red's mouth.

'It should only take a second or two.' Ethic told the librarian.

'Oh . . . that's better, much better.' Red said after a moment. 'Thanks.'

Heading back to the car park, Red put the Librarian's card in her pocket. 'You were able to get a photo of the screen?'

Steve laughed, 'Get a photo? . . . I could have printed the page out and rewritten it and nobody would have noticed. That was a proper diversion. Am I getting one?' He nodded at the round tin that Ethnic was still holding.

'What do you think; we did most of the work?' Ethnic asked Red.
'Most of the work? - I took the photo and she said oh.' Steve protested.
'That was acting,' Red turned to Ethnic. 'Go on and I'll have another.'
'We've got to stop using Skittles they don't last.' Ethnic told them passing the tin around.
'Major Sam James, Ty Bryn, bottom lane, Nantyderry.' Steve told them.

Red was using one of the self-propelling chairs from the school; these folded up and fitted easily into the back of Ethnic's Fiesta. Getting out of Abergavenny however turned out to be far more complicated than expected. They left the car park and soon found themselves stuck in a queue of vehicles.
The car radio told them that a group protesting at Trump's election was placing a banner 'Bridges not Walls' on the side of Llanfoist Bridge.
Steve flicked the radio off and adopted a passable American accent. 'Just in shock news from Washington, Donald Trump's election to president has been cancelled; I repeat the election is off. News of the Llanfoist demonstration reached the Whitehouse this hour and Trump was heard saying to his advisors, how can I possibly go on now, it's over, it's all

over.'
'Why penalise us - all they're doing is just jamming up the town, how's that going to change anything?' Ethnic wasn't seeing the funny side.
'So we going to this guys house now?' Steve was Welsh again.
'Yep.' Red answered.
'Where the hell is Nantyderry?' Ethnic asked exasperated.
'Bottom of Penperlenni.'
'Oh yeah great help where the hell is Penper . . . penper?' Ethnic's Welsh was a work in progress.
'Penperlenni - It's on the 4042 head for Ponty.' Red told him.
'How are going to do this?' Steve asked.
'We'll cross that bridge when we come to it.'
'That's if we ever get over this one!' Ethnic moaned.

After some more queuing and then some driving back and forth through country lanes they arrived at a small detached Georgian cottage in an idyllic narrow lane. The boys helped Red out of the car and lifted her up the three stone steps and onto a flat and level stone garden path.
'We could just tell him the truth.' Steve suggested under his breath as they approached the front door.
Red glanced back at him narrowing her eyes.

They came to a large blue wooden front door. A sign, with oddly spaced lettering, appeared to say TB but closer examination revealed it had originally said Ty Bryn before the rest of the letters had fallen off.

Steve rang the bell.

A few moments later, a tall thin elderly lady, narrow glasses, hair in a bun, opened the door and looked with some surprise at her visitors.

'Yes.' She answered.

'Could we see Major Samuel James please?' Red asked with her best smile.

'Major Samantha James' the woman replied.

'Oh - I see erm is that you? Are you?'

'Yes.'

'Oh right Hi, we're from Millbrook Comprehensive we're erm cataloging the library bequest, which means visiting all of the local libraries that have sample books. We understand from Abergavenny that you have . . . the . . . what was it Steve? (Red faltered under the woman's stare).

'The Argonath four.' Steve replied coolly.'

'That's right the Argonath volume four.'

The woman stared back silently for a few moments. 'If that were the case then surely the school would have contacted the libraries and arranged for all the books to be there.' She said sounding more than a little suspicious. 'Furthermore the library would not have given you my name or address, have you not heard of data protection? – Now tell me the truth.'

Steve had had enough, 'A gardener was killed in our school, his body was found drained of blood.'

'Oh right so you think there's a vampire loose in your school and you want the Argonath to tell you how to destroy it.' She replied sarcastically.

Red realised that Steve had been right. 'Not a vampire, the third Argonath spoke of a sorcerer, Gregory of Caldicot, when ambushed at Tretower he conjured a monster to defeat his enemies. The story's a myth, a fable, complete tosh, except, for one thing.'

'Go on.' The Major was suddenly interested.

'Except for the description of the creature. There are elements that would have made no sense to the people of the time but a modern biologist would recognise . . .'

'That it was based on something real but something unknown to science.' The Major finished, the suspicion had melted from her face to be replaced by a warm and genuine smile. 'I've made you sandwiches, are Tuna and Sweet corn okay?' She turned on her heel, and disappeared into the house leaving the kids staring after her in amazement.

'Sorry about the step.' She shouted back.

Inside the door was a small step, Steve and Ethnic expertly bumped Red down the step and into the house. Inside it was cosy but a little cluttered.

They followed the Major into a large open kitchen. Three

plates of sandwiches were on the table next to a big bottle of Lemonade. Beside these was a large battered leather bound book.

'You were expecting us? - How could you be?' Red began.

'I'd asked the Library to contact me if anyone asked for the Argonath. You'll forgive me but the three of you are, um, distinctive. Justine at the Library told me that you'd asked about the book and what happened afterwards, then twenty minutes later a car with 2 boys and a red headed girl is driving up and down my lane.

'Yeah we had a job finding you, did it ever occur to you to put the house name on the gate? - You'd be a lot easier to find.' Ethnic said.

'Maybe I don't want to be found.' She told him with a mischievous smile as her eyes fell on Red who was staring at the book.

'The Argonath volumes speak of many mysteries and you're right a lot of it is complete tosh but there's truth in there as well.' The Major began, 'The trick is to tell fact from fiction. The story of Gregory of Caldicot is famous as one of the first references to vampires in literature. Gregory was what we'd call today a con artist. He was a habitual gambler who by chance acquired some primitive Chinese fireworks. He used these to convince people that he was a sorcerer supreme, then he'd take them for every penny he could. One day he deceived one of the mayors of Monmouth a man called

Raven, he got the location of a great treasure hidden within the town. Gregory made off with the treasure and Raven realised he'd been deceived. Raven got together a group of sheriff's, four ruthless men; he knew would stop at nothing, to follow Gregory and bring back his head. They caught up with him at Tretower . . .'

Red took up the story. 'In a long barn in the middle of a valley they waited until nightfall and when they were sure Gregory was asleep, they crept into the barn to kill him but something went wrong.' She looked to the Major.

'Yes the barn was suddenly consumed in flames and a swarm of bats attacked the men. All four were killed, their bodies drained of blood.'

'Vampire bats?' Steve suggested.

'Not in Wales mate and it wasn't just the bats.' Red answered.

'No the locals saw something else in the flames,' the Major continued. 'Like unto a woman with glistening skin and of a hideous twisted face.'

'The creature's heartbeat could be seen in her throat and everything she touched was left covered in slime, a slime which consumed any living thing that touched it.' Red told them.

'Do what? - You're kidding right?' Ethnic spluttered.

'Several of the villagers laid hands on her, tried to grab her but her skin burnt their hands. All were dead within the hour and all of those dead were in rapture.' The major gestured towards the waiting sandwiches, the boys needed no further encouragement.

'In rapture?' Steve queried through a mouthful of sandwich.

'They died with smiles on their faces. 'Red and the Major answered together.

Steve and Ethnic exchanged glances.

'Oh Bugger.' Steve said quietly.

'Okay if you've read the story why do you need this book?' Ethnic too shared his question with a sandwich.

The Major answered before Red could. 'Because your friend has obviously worked out how Argonath distinguished fact from fiction, haven't you my dear?'

Red leaned forward in her chair, 'Remember what Mary was always saying about the gospels in R.E.?'

Ethnic and Steve looked blank but the major nodded.

'The same events, seen by different people with different viewpoints, guys don't you ever listen?'

The boys stared blankly back, 'In R.E. not always.' Ethnic admitted.

'In most lessons, not always.' Steve elaborated.

'In our defence though we usually ask you afterwards.

'Ethnic looked at Steve who nodded.

Red shook her head, 'the accounts vary but the facts remain the same. The differences prove not disprove, like witnesses in court that differ in the details but agree on the facts that matter.'

The Major took over. 'You are correct of course; Argonath always got as many different accounts as he could. He'd put them together and see where they agreed and where they differed.'

'But Argonath collected these accounts over a period of time, putting together the volumes as he went. Consequently we often find the same event in several volumes. By comparing these you have a chance to work out fact from fiction.' Red explained like it was all the most obvious thing in the world.

'So does volume four add anything to volume three?' Steve asked through a mouthful of another sandwich.

The Major picked up the book and started flicking through the pages. 'I'll make some photocopies for you but in a nutshell the first account tells that Gregory left Tretower in flames. He took the road to Brecon accompanied by a hideous creature but he never arrived. He died on route and the creature carried his body off into the mountains.' She found the page that she wanted and placed the open book on the table in front of Red and pointed to a paragraph near the top of the page. Red leaned over the book to read as the Major continued. 'The second account is pretty much the same as that in the third volume except that it ends differently, it says that Gregory was attacked and wounded by the creature. He was carried into the village where he was nursed by a widow who knew how to treat his wounds. She covered them with white clay and bound them tightly. In return Gregory told her what the treasure of Monmouth was and where he'd hidden it. He promised that when he was well he'd share it with her and ordered her to tell nobody. But the sickness returned claiming him and her as well but not before she'd hidden the location of the treasure in a local church.' She finished.

'Oh well that clears everything up nicely.' Ethnic said sarcastically.

Well let's see if I can help. Millbrook has all the Argonath volumes apart from volumes two, four and seven.' The Major answered. 'Volume four is here, volume seven is lost and volume two was destroyed in Stalingrad during the Second World War. There were several copies made however, all scattered across Eastern Europe and all of these have a drawing called the widow's map. Nobody realised the significance before, because volumes three and four were only discovered when the bequest became known. The books are historical oddities rather than rarities; they're not worth a great deal so there was little publicity.'

Red raised her head from the book, 'Nico, the gardener was from Eastern Europe.'

'Clever girl, yes Romania,' the Major answered.

'Not Transylvania then?' Steve quipped.

'Was he looking for the treasure?' Red asked.

'Undoubtedly, but not in that hole.'
'He couldn't have been digging because there was no loose soil.' Red mused looking out through the kitchen windows to a pretty cottage garden.
'No his body was moved there,' the Major nodded.
'So hang on, what killed him?' Steve moved to his final sandwich.
'And who moved the body?' Ethnic added.
'There's a more relevant question,' the Major said.
'How can a creature from medieval history be wondering around Wales? And what on earth is it?' Red said quietly.
'Right!' said the Major, bringing to Steve's delight, a huge Battenberg cake to the table. 'So what would a modern biologist make of the description? - Let's see how clever you really are?'
Red, noticing that Steve and Ethnic had finished their sandwiches with gusto and were eyeing the one's set aside for her, grabbed one. 'The heartbeat in the throat is Gular pumping.' She took a small bite out of the sandwich.
'Gular what?' Ethnic was rarely able to concentrate for long in Biology.
Steve raised his phone, drumming the keys with his fingers. 'Gular pumping, the sole means of inflating the lungs in amphibians. It's accomplished by expanding and contracting the entire throat to pump air, rather than just relying upon the mouth. This method is used by all air-breathing

amphibians, Wikipedia.' He read aloud.

Red took over. 'In Medieval England, there were a couple of species of frogs and Toads. The frogs were your basic common frogs, smooth moist skin, variable in colour. The Toads had warty, dry skin and were generally grey brown. The Toads had large glands on the back of the neck which produced a milky substance that made them unpleasant to eat but that was about it. These sandwiches are delicious - Thanks!'

'Go on,' the Major said watching Red with interest.

'We now know that Frogs and Toads around the world are far more varied than this. Many have sophisticated chemical defences.'

'Poison arrow frogs,' Ethnic remembered that bit.

Red's approach to her sandwich was completely different to the boys who'd demolished theirs outright. Red ate hers daintily taking care not to drop crumbs on the book. 'Yep and more besides, as science discovered more species, so we discovered just how varied and ingenious they are. There were no amphibians in medieval England with poisonous burning skin, there was no precedent but today we have a number of species that have this. Gregory's creature in the book is an Amphibian, a cold blooded, air breathing Amphibian.'

'Whoa hang on, Frogs are tiny they eat insects, they don't have teeth, they swallow stuff.' Ethnic knew that bit.

Steve juggled his phone and a second slice of Battenberg. 'The Goliath frog from Africa can reach a weight in excess of 3.25kg.'

'Pounds and ounces if you please.' The Major demanded.

'Sorry er can reach a weight in excess of 7lb the size of a house cat.'

'Okay that's a big Frog.' Ethnic conceded.

Steve was hitting his stride now. 'The Japanese Hellbender salamander can be as long as 30 inches.'

'Okay, big Newt but it's still nowhere near as big as the thing in the book. And frogs don't drink blood.' Ethnic said helping himself to a slice of cake.

'There is a Vampire flying frog.' Red told him.

'Rhacophorus vampyrus a Vietnamese tree frog discovered in 2008, so named because –'the Major turned to Steve.

'The Tadpoles have fangs, 'Steve was quick with his phone. 'National Geographic.' He added looking expectantly to the others and noticing that there was still some Battenberg left.

'Help yourself,' the Major told him.

'Okay Tadpoles maybe but frogs don't have Teeth!' Ethnic was sure about this.

'Actually mate, 'Red began.'

'African Bullfrogs are one of several species that have sharp teeth and bite humans when provoked or handled by people. The hairy frog, Trichobatrachus robustus also known as the horror frog is able to break its own bones to produce claws ...' Steve was in full flow now.

'Gimmie that!' Ethnic tried to grab Steve's phone but Steve simply held it out higher than Ethnic could reach.

'The point is Amphibians are highly adaptable so that as conditions change they're able to adapt and change with them.' Red cut in.

'But not to turn into something out of a Horror film.' Ethnic protested.

The major took a slim green box from the worktop behind her and slid the contents (half a dozen mince pies) onto a plate. As she passed one to Steve, Ethnic pounced and grabbed Steve's phone.

'And the book said the creature was like a woman.' Ethnic taunted Steve waving his phone triumphantly at him. 'And . . .' it was Ethnic's turn to use Steve's phone. 'There are no known, living or fossil bipedal amphibians.'

'But in pre-history there were many bipedal lizards large and small.' The Major pointed out.

'Major are you suggesting that this creature comes from pre-history?' Red asked.

'No Dinosaurs survived at all!' Ethnic was grappling with Steve for the phone.

'But other creatures did Crocodiles, Turtles, Sturgeon.' Red said thoughtfully.

Steve had got Ethnic off the floor now tucked under one arm and he was trying to retrieve his phone by tickling him. 'And

Coelacanth.'
'And Coelacanth,' the Major conceded.
Red frowned, 'Okay so in prehistoric times there may have been a large bipedal amphibian unknown to science, but how could it have still been alive in medieval times? - This is what I can't understand; I can accept that such a creature could have existed. The details described in the Argonath also persuade me that the writer had seen such a creature but how? And what's worse is that the body found at our school suggests that it's still here but that's impossible.'
'Aestivation.' The Major said quietly.
Nobody said anything they just waited for Steve who'd got his phone back. 'Aestivation or æstivation (from Latin: aestas) is a state of animal dormancy, similar to hibernation, characterized by inactivity and a lowered metabolic rate, that is entered in response to high temperatures and arid conditions.'
Red was sceptical, 'Okay but that's for a few months maybe a year or two.'
The Major picked up a large old fashioned kettle and walked over to the sink. 'It's not unreasonable to assume that once there was a large bipedal amphibian unknown to the fossil record. Many species of Dinosaurs have been classified on the basis of the remains or fragments of remains of a single specimen. The creature would have been high on the food chain, a predator, a very specialised one. There are

always fewer predators than prey, so it's rare. The climate at the time is unstable so the species adapts as it's been designed to. When the world is hot and dry it buries itself in a water-tight mucus cocoon. As the world changes few of even these would survive but maybe one or two did.' She said whilst she filled the kettle.

Red nodded accepting her argument. 'You've obviously been wondering about this, may I ask what your interest is?'

'I used to work for an obscure government department, long gone now – cutbacks.' She replied without bitterness. She lifted the teapot up to see if any of them wanted tea but all eyes were on the lemonade bottle. 'Go on help yourselves, there's no need to stand on ceremony. There are glasses in that cupboard.'

Steve attended to the glasses as Ethnic swung the lemonade bottle up from the table and battled with the bottle top.

'We investigated the odd and the unusual, things that baffled the police and other authorities,' the Major continued.

'Like Men in black?' Ethnic asked wiping lemonade from his shirt.

'More Ladies in tweed – I'm officially retired but I still keep my ear to the ground and I still have my contacts. In October 2007 the Monmouthshire & Brecon canal burst its banks at Gilwern just outside Abergavenny. It was such a severe break that a 16 mile stretch of the canal was out of action until the following March.'

'I remember that, it was on the news, there was mud everywhere.' Steve passed the glasses to Ethnic who filled them with what remained of the lemonade.

'Yeah they had to evacuate some of the residents didn't they?' Red said accepting a glass from Ethnic.

'Yes ten people were rescued but that's beside the point. The following morning a local farmer found two of his sheep dead. No sign of distress or attack but . . .'

'They had been drained of blood?'

The major nodded, 'A local copper tipped off one of my colleagues so we kept it out of the Abergavenny Chronicle. But as we researched it and dug a little deeper we discovered that this had happened before. Not often, only a few times in the whole of the previous century but always one or two sheep and always after a flood.'

'Oh bloody hell,' Ethnic spluttered.

'Yes young man, oh bloody hell.' The Major replied with a half smile.

'Then we've got to tell someone, the police, the government.' Ethic said as he wiped down the table top.

'And who do you think would believe us?' The Major asked flatly.

'Like you said you've got contacts, government agency folk and all.' Steve suggested.

'Sorry no, my contacts are people on the ground, people in

the community. Our department was audited and discredited. In government circles I'm a relic, nobody is going to listen to me. The only thing I have now my dears.' The Major paused clipping the lid onto the kettle and plugging it in. 'Is you.'

'Us!?' Red spluttered, 'What can we do?'

'Look what you've done already, you're looking and you're thinking and you've got further than anyone else has. The Police have got nowhere and you three have already worked out at least some of what's happened. You know something that scientists and experts do not. If it was just the creature you'd be almost there but there's something else at work here, something that complicates matters.'

Red turned to Steve and Ethnic who both grinned, 'Beats treasure hunts' Ethnic observed.

Red turned back to the Major, 'Okay Major, what do you want us to do?'

'You give me your email addresses, you stay in touch and you read my dear. Most of the remaining volumes are at your school. We're missing something and it's something that must be in one of those books.' The Major left the room taking the Argonath volume then returned a minute or two later with an A3 brown envelope. 'Here are the photocopies I promised and the map.'

'You've got the widows map?'

'Yes but its incomplete. The widow had a son and had left

the map for him. It has directions from a starting point to the treasure's location. But it's a code that the mother knew the son would be able to understand. There's an X, yes X marks the spot but we don't know if it's the start or the finish. All the landmarks are represented as triangles and circles. The only other thing written on it is the number seven. No place names, no directions, just a letter and a number.' She passed the photocopied map to Red who looked at it and frowned.

'I'd better do a bit more reading then,' Red said.

The Major took her hand, 'Keep in touch and whatever you do, don't do anything rash!'

Three

Red spent so much time in the school library that she had her own desk or rather desks, as two of the old fashioned wooden square desks, salvaged from an old storeroom had been jammed together and rammed into the corner. Beside Red's desk was the table bearing the Libraries ancient computer and printer. The computer boasted Windows 98 and dial up internet so most people ignored it but the monitor screen was much larger than the school laptops and the internet on this machine was not part of the school's intranet.

Red had spent all of her free time for the best part of a fortnight going carefully through the Argonath volumes and associated books looking for any material that she might have missed previously. The conversation with the Major and in particular the discovery of the map had provided a real focus for her enquiring mind and inquisitive nature. This was now a proper treasure hunt, it was as if everything else had been leading up, building up to this.

Problem was she wasn't getting anywhere, after hours of reading and cross checking she'd found very little.

There were several references to a widow who appeared to be a musician of some kind and references also to an 'Angels gifts.' The links were tenuous to say the least; this widow saved her village with a Bell or a rattle, no mentions of maps or treasure let alone monstrous amphibians. What made it more frustrating was that the author was referring to another longer more detailed account which had since become lost. The angel's gifts were listed in another Argonath but here also the list was incomplete and not exactly helpful.

Firstly it spoke of a key that couldn't be seen to open a door that wasn't there. A clock that took you backwards to go forwards and sandals that could take you instantly to anywhere you could picture in your mind. Then there were the 'Angels tears' these would heal any ailment but at a cost and it could turn clay to white clay and lead to Silver. The 'Angels sword' could kill any enemy but it always cut both ways. Finally the 'Angels eye' was tiny but if you wore it on your finger and looked into it, it would show you the love of your life.

The link here was the white clay, she'd never heard of it before but it was in the angels list as well as in the Argonath account of Gregory and the creature.

Red stared glumly at the list as Steve and Ethnic arrived with provisions.

The boys had decided long ago that when it came to research the best approach was leave it all to Red, she knew what she was doing and she excelled at it. They on the other hand, took on their role equally seriously. They would keep

Red supplied with copious quantities of sandwiches and coke whenever and wherever they were needed.

Red thanked them and tore open a triangular cardboard packet with the letters BLT emblazoned upon it. 'How was the run?' she asked noticing Steve's tracksuit and the tiny drops of sweat that were still dotting his forehead.

'You know the boathouse down by the bridge.'

'Blimey you went a way,' Red mumbled through a mouthful of bacon and lettuce.

'You know the steps down to the river?'

'Yep . . . who slipped?'

'Jones four, from the top, hit every step on the way down then straight into the river.'

'Blimey – was he alright?'

'Me and Roger fished him out, we thought he was dead at first but Stevie found a pulse so we carried him back. We were all supposed to wait in town for the bus to pick us up but Kenny couldn't start it.'

'You carried him from Monmouth?'

'Yeah, he wasn't that heavy and we took it in turns.' Steve snorted.

'Didn't anyone call an ambulance?'' Ethnic asked not taking his eyes from Red's notebook which he was reading.

'Yeah me and Rog were going to but he came round for a few moments and said he'd be okay if we could get him back to the garden centre.'

'The garden centre why there?' Red asked removing a slice of tomato (which she hated) from her sandwich and handing it to Steve.

'That was the meeting point with the other running group.' Steve said cheerfully chewing the tomato. 'Lottie was in the other running group,' he added with a sly grin to Ethnic who smirked.

'Lottie's two years above him,' Red took another bite of her sandwich before fishing the final piece of tomato from the remaining corner and handing it to Ethnic. 'He doesn't think . . . ?'

'He does, or rather he did.'

'Hasn't Lottie just done a first aid course?' Ethnic asked finishing his piece of Tomato.

'Now you're getting it.' Steve grinned.

'Yes I remember now, she was telling us all how she'd done CPR on a dummy.' Ethnic laughed, 'and . . .'

'Jones four was in the common room at the time.' Steve finished for him.

Red stared at Steve as he started a game on his phone, 'Are you saying the little idiot fell down the steps and into the river just so that Lottie would do CPR on him.'

'Yeah he was carrying a pop bottle too when he fell and fair play to him he didn't let go of it til he landed.' Steve said without looking up.

Red slowly shook her head.

'A sword that cuts both ways?' Ethnic asked raising his head from Red's list.

Red's attention was drawn to the window as an ambulance, siren wailing and blue lights flashing pulled into the school courtyard.

'Double edged sword isn't it.' Steve announced.

'Yeah obviously, so how come they never just say that.' Ethnic raised his hands in the air as Red watched a pair of paramedic's race from the ambulance into the school. 'Everything's got to be a mystery, hasn't it, got to be a riddle.' He continued, 'Here listen to this.'

Steve raised his eyes from his phone, as the bomb he was trying to defuse in the game started flashing.

'A key that can't be seen to open a door that isn't there.' Ethnic read out.

'Aw come on that's stupid,' Steve agreed. 'If you can't see the key, how you going to pick it up? It's hard enough to find keys as it is.'

'So Jones wasn't injured at all?' Red interrupted.

'No didn't say that, turns out he'd broken a leg but he was just pretending to be unconscious.'

'He broke his leg?'

'It was a lot of steps.'

Red saw one of the paramedics run back to the ambulance and jump into the back, a moment later he jumped out and ran back into the school carrying an oxygen bottle.

'And when you've got the key, if the lock's not there how can you put the key in it?' Ethnic was sat next to Steve now his attention divided between Steve's game and Red's list.

'Is Jones four asthmatic?' Red asked.

'Yeah he had an asthma attack after Lottie beat him up.'

'Didn't you look to see if he had an inhaler?'

Steve looked up from his game, 'Course we looked for his inhaler, none of us are stupid.' He replied slightly wounded, 'We knew what to do; his inhaler was in his back pocket, so we used it.'

A loud flash and bang rang out from Steve's phone.

'Bugger!' he grimaced.

'Should have cut the Blue one,' Ethnic told him helpfully.

'Did the inhaler sort him out?'

'Well no actually,' Steve mumbled restarting his game, 'which Blue, this one?'

'No the other one, the one on the right,' Ethnic said confidently, 'No not that right the other right.'

There was another flash and bang from Steve's phone.

'What happened?'

'Well see, we dragged Lottie off him, got the inhaler into his mouth and pressed the top down but –'

'But?'

'Been in the river hadn't it, he just got a mouthful of muddy water.' Steve turned to Ethnic, 'You said the blue.'

'Yeah but after you cut the yellow.'

'You didn't mention the yellow.'

'Everyone knows you cut the yellow first.'

Steve started the game again, 'On the plus side, he did get to snog Lottie that's not bad for a first year.'

'No - the other yellow,' Ethnic said jabbing Steve's phone with his finger.

'She beat him up!'

'He said it was worth it and it livened up the garden centre cafe I can tell you.'

'You took him into the cafe to give him CPR?'

'Red we were gasping,' Steve bit back outraged as the bomb exploded again. 'None of us had had a drink had we?'

'Why didn't you take drinks with you?'

'We didn't want to be carrying all those little plastic bottles around with us, so we took one of the big industrial catering bottles from the canteen, filled it with pop and orange and took that for all of us.'

Red stared at Steve open-mouthed, 'Are you insane? – those bottles are huge who in their right mind would be stupid enough to go on a run carrying . . . oh dear god' a look of horror spread across her face. 'Who was carrying the bottle?' She whispered.

Steve stared back at red, 'Jones four obviously.'

'He's a first year, those bottles weigh a ton!'

'He volunteered.'

There was another flash and bang from Steve's phone.

'This is dumb my brother completed Bomb-man months ago I know that sequence was right.' Ethnic scratched his head, 'How do these things tie in with the giant frog?' he asked Red who was watching the tiny figure of Jones four being stretchered into the ambulance, a large oxygen mask covering most of his face but his huge smile was obvious even from distance.

'White clay,' Red replied distracted.

'Oh yeah, Clay into white clay, blimey is this all you got?'

'This is Bomb-man three.'

'Oh well that's why the blue didn't work, it's orange and green on Bomb-man three.'

Red watched the Ambulance bolt out of the school lights flashing and siren screaming.

'There isn't a green and there's three oranges.' Steve protested.

Red looked at the boys and slowly shook her head.

The following day the Major got back in touch; she had some new information and suggested that they meet up at the Garden centre cafe near the school.

Millbrook Garden Centre was in fact just across the road from the school. Looking from the road the car park was in front of the main building and the coffee shop/restaurant was a separate building to the right of the car park as you entered.

There was a ramp beside the steps up to the cafe and the three of them got in and got a table at the back of the room without too much difficulty. The Major arrived soon afterwards, giving them a cheery wave as she ordered a cup of tea. Steve and Ethnic walked over to where she stood.
'Can we tempt you to an ice cream Major they're really good.' Steve asked.
'Later perhaps dear.'
'Later?'
She pulled an old fashioned round fob watch from a pocket and glanced at it, 'July.'
The three of them returned to the table and Red.
The Major leant forward in her seat and spoke quietly so that only Red and the boys could hear, even though the cafe was almost deserted. 'Your gardener was Nicolae Bogaz he was 25 and from Luncani in Romania. He wasn't a gardener he was a researcher at the University of Bacau. He came over to this country last year with three other men.'
'Do you know who they are?' Red asked.
'Not yet but I will.' The Major told them. 'Now what are you three doing on Saturday?'
Red looked at the boys both of whom shook their heads.
'Nothing, why?'
'Could you three meet me here at 9.30am?' The Major handed Red a slip of paper.
On the Paper - **Bryn Du, Maryport Street, Usk** was neatly

written.

'Bryn du?' Ethnic queried, reading over Red's shoulder.

'Means Black Hill,' the Major told him. 'This was the house that Nicolae rented,' she explained. 'The police have searched it but there was little to be found, a few possessions food and clothes, that sort of thing.'

'Aren't the other two who came over with him living there?' Steve asked.

'No it was just him.'

'Do you think the Police missed something?' Red asked.

'One of the buildings in your school is a large maintenance shed.' The Major said sipping her tea.

'Aye that's where they keep the mowers and stuff,' Ethnic replied.

'Inside as well as the mowers and stuff is a row of lockers. When Nicolae was killed he didn't have his keys on him, they were safe in his locker. The night before his body turned up somebody tried to break into the maintenance shed but failed.'

'How can you know that? We don't even know that and it's our school!' Ethnic protested over a spoonful of Rum punch Ice cream.

'The police didn't find anything other than what they expected to find.' The Major continued ignoring Ethnic's question. 'So they're releasing the house back to the letting agents as the landlord wants a new tenant in as soon as possible. The house will be open for viewing from Saturday and I've told the agents that i'm interested in it for my granddaughter and her friends.' Her voice changed to an excellent impersonation of a doddery old grandmother. 'My granddaughter's studying at the new university in Newport you know, we're all terribly proud. She wants somewhere in Usk as she's always liked the town.'

'It's all the pubs,' Ethic observed earning himself a thump from Red.

The Major continued undaunted. 'We'd like to come on Saturday but I'm not sure exactly what time she and her friends can get down. So if you could give me a long slot for viewing that would be much appreciated.'

'How long have we got?'

'Until noon.'

'What is it that we're looking for Major?' Steve asked.

'Nicolae spent quite a bit of time in several libraries, especially Newport, Caldicot and Abergavenny. I've spoken to a few of the assistants all of whom remember him writing copious notes. None of his notebooks were found and somebody wanted to get his keys.'

'9.30 Saturday morning then.' Red grinned finishing her coke, 'Bryn Du, Maryport Street.'

'Yes see you then, oh and Ethnic, the name sign is on the gate.' She told them as she left.

'She called me Ethnic,' Ethnic said nudging Steve.

They arrived the following Saturday and soon spotted the Majors battered green mini parked outside the house they were looking for (the name was indeed on the gate). The Major was halfway up the path and stopped when she saw them arrive. 'Sorry about the steps' she called.

'It's okay, I've got them well trained,' Red called back holding onto the armrests for dear life as the boy's hauled her and her chair up the steps.

The major was wearing a pair of really tatty overalls under her trim blue coat and carrying a large hold-all. She twisted the key in the lock and carefully pushed the door open. 'Don't touch anything as you come in.' She advised.

Immediately inside the door there was a narrow staircase in front and an internal door to the right.

'Okay Red you search upstairs, we'll do down here.' Ethnic said.

'Nothing like a good joke.' Red replied wearily.

'Wait for it,' Steve told nobody in particular as he helped Red back through the internal door into a small magnolia lounge.

'And that was nothing like a good joke.' Red finished.

First things first put these on (the Major handed each of them a pair of thin flesh coloured latex gloves) as she did so they noticed that she was already wearing a pair.

'There's been a development,' the Major whispered

although nobody else was in the house. 'Last night somebody broke in, they were seen by someone in the house across the road. Police were here in 5 minutes but they'd scarpered. The agent said there's a broken upstairs window at the back which will be fixed Monday. She said that nothing was taken because there was nothing left to take.'

'Do you reckon they found what they were looking for?' Red asked looking at the bare walls and shelves.

'Was it Bono who broke in then?' Steve asked causing Ethnic to smile.

'Hopefully not,' the Major replied.

The Major was soon outlining their strategy; she and Steve would start upstairs. Ethnic and Red would search the lounge and kitchen.

Ethnic left the others and wandered into the kitchen.

He could still hear the Major's voice in the background saying that it could take them hours and even then they might not find anything.

The kitchen was crowded with cupboards and units, the walls in the kitchen were pale green and the skirting boards were a faded gloss white. The walls had obviously been carefully over-painted and masked over the skirting. Above all of the skirting boards there was a neat join of the white and green layers. All of them, that was, except one.

Ethic knelt and carefully examined this skirting board which was beside the fridge; it had a thin black line, as thin as a hair, running along its length.

'It couldn't be this easy surely,' Ethnic said quietly to himself.

'Major do you have a screwdriver in that bag of yours?' He called.

'Phillips or Flat?' She called back.

'Flat, bigger the better'.

The Major appeared brandishing a large flat headed screw driver. 'Here what do you . . .?'

'This skirting board's been moved and put back.' He was kneeling beside it looking along its length.

The Major knelt beside him and did the same.

'You're right, oh well spotted (she patted him on the back.) Look can you see there's a fine film of sawdust on the top and along the join with the floor. After the police finished the agents got the cleaners in, I'll bet one of them knocked it with the vacuum.' She nodded towards a large grey and white Vacuum cleaner stood in the corner.

'Just enough to move the sawdust he used to hide the gap or . . .'

'Or the burglar found it last night.' Red said rolling into the room followed by Steve.

'He would have had to know it was here, he had five minutes, he'd never have found it in that short a time otherwise.' The Major mused.

'I found it in five minutes.' Ethnic pointed out.

'Yes but that's because you're a Genius!' The Major laughed ruffling his hair. She went back for her bag and took out another screwdriver and a torch.

Ethnic raised himself to his full height and puffed his chest out. 'Y'see Genius, she said so.' He told Red and Steve who giggled quietly.

Soon they were carefully prising the skirting board from the wall.

'Remember we need to leave this place as we found it,' the Major reminded them.

Initially the inner wall behind appeared empty but then as the Major slowly shone her torch back and forth they noticed something jammed against the far corner at the back. Steve lay flat on the kitchen floor and stretched his arm in as far as it would go. He was eventually able to pull out a black plastic bin bag which they carefully opened.

Inside a quick glance revealed notebooks and many sheets of paper. The notebooks and pages were all covered in writing. A little was in English but the rest was Romanian and Hungarian.

'I've got a translation ap. on my phone,' Steve suggested.

'No there's too much,' the Major replied flicking through a pile of papers. 'We'll need an expert and I know one. Look let's get this place back to how it was, I'll drop the keys back and tell them I'll let them know. Then once this lot is sorted I can email you what we find. In the meantime you three can have your Saturday back.

Outside the house Red and the boys waved to the Major as they headed for both of their cars. Parked across the road was a black (and quite battered) Ford transit. The driver was clearly watching the four of them as they drove away.

A few days later Red was still puzzling over the map, she had the maddening feeling that the answer was staring her in the face but she just couldn't see it. She sat poring over the map as Steve, Ethnic and Roger tried to play keepie up with a flat football.

Roger lived opposite Steve, all through primary school they were the best of friends but a game of D&D had brought both youngsters to blows and neither one had spoken to the other for four years. Red and Roger's sister Vicky had finally brokered a truce between the two, who were now able to tolerate each other's company fairly amicably (provided nobody mentioned D&D). The four of them were in the sixth form common room with four new pupils who had been transferred into the school for various reasons. These had been given the tour by Mr. Dobbs, who then left them in the common room. Red and the boys were to have an informal chat with them and answer any questions that they might have before they were taken to their classes. All they had to do was put them at their ease.

Red smiled at the newbie's two boys Peter and Mike were clearly her age and two younger girls Rachel, who Red guessed would be about twelve and Jane who she put at fourteen or so.

The sixth form common room had been equipped and decorated by the students themselves. Over the years a really eclectic set of furniture and fixtures had been collected. If you changed your furniture in the Millbrook area and you had a kid in the school, this was where the old chairs and sofa's would end up. There were a dozen armchairs, all different styles and colours and four equally varied settees, two-seaters and three-seaters all jumbled together. The large room had two different carpets side by side on the floor, one a deep plain burgundy the other, a flowery rust and lime green combination. To complete the ensemble the windows in the room had had the original blinds replaced with curtains (the only ones in the whole school). The four windows shared three different sets of curtains, none of which were quite the right size. The whole effect of the room was striking to say the least but it managed to feel relaxed and cosy also.

'As schools go it's not that bad,' Steve told the newbie's, 'If there's a weakness it's work experience.' he added to a chorus of agreement from the other's in the room.

'What are the teacher's like?' Peter, the eldest of the group asked eagerly.
'Most of them are fine but that Mr. Powell has his moments,' Ethnic observed thoughtfully.
'Yeah and Mrs. Blake can be a pain on times,' Red added.
'Then there's Mr. Watkins and Mr. Bryn.' Roger said, getting nods of agreement from Red and the boys.'
'Yeah, Mr. Bryn's in charge of stationary, he's a happy soul,' Ethnic told them sarcastically. 'When you need a new exercise book you'll have to see him. He'll want to see your old one first and he'll want to check you've not ripped out any of the pages. If you have . . .' Ethnic stopped speaking and slowly drew his finger across his throat.' The two younger girls started to look a little concerned.
'Then there's Mr. James,' Steve said.
'And Mr. Brooks, he's been in prison twice' Roger added.
'Mr. Gates is a right Dragon,' Ethnic said.
'Oh and Mrs. Fields and Mrs. Potter,' Steve continued.
'Guys' Red could see that the two younger girls were taking all of this a little too seriously now and tried to reign in the boys who were approaching full flow.
'Mr. Black,' Ethnic said ignoring the interruption.
'Yeah and that new teaching assistant's a bit weird, the one with the pipe and hairpiece, what's his name?' Roger asked.
'The one with the limp or the one who supports Watford?' Ethnic asked.

'No not them, the other one, the one who threw Taff down the stairs?' Roger told him.
'That's Mr. Jones and he supports Palace' Steve cut in helpfully.
'Guys Taff fell down the stairs.'
'Then there's Mr. Martin, he's a reformed Cannibal.'
'Well they say he's reformed but Williams five said that Lennie's mate's friend sneaked a look in his lunchbox one morning and he saw that inside his sausage rolls were-'
'GUYS' Red didn't shout very often but she was more than capable when the need arose. Her eyes flicked to the two girls who were both near to tears.
Steve had guilt, 'it's ok we're only messing with you, the teachers are fine.' He said as breezily as he could, 'Mostly.'
Ethnic agreed, 'Yeah, you'll soon have em' all under your thumb, they're only Teachers after all.'
Roger and Steve nodded their agreement.
'There's only one teacher you really need to watch,' Red told them gently.
'Only one that you should be really wary of,' Steve added helpfully.
'Only one that you should fear,' Roger contributed.
'Roger!'
Peter and the girls turned their eyes to Red, 'Who?' the youngest girl whispered looking frankly terrified.
'Miss Wheeler,' Red, Roger and the boys answered in

unison.

'We saw her this morning, she seemed rather nice.' The smallest girl told them.

Steve, Ethnic and Roger all looked at each other and smiled.

'Yep that's about right; she generally seems okay – at first.' Steve told them.

'My dad said that the first time he met her,' Ethnic sat back in his tatty but comfortable blue and red check armchair. 'Seems quite reasonable he said, didn't know what I was on about he said. Then he met her that second time on parents evening.'

Steve and Roger nodded grimly, 'Yes I remember that, poor guy he was in a bit of a state wasn't he?' Steve said solemnly.

'What happened,' Rachel, the younger of the two girls, gasped wide eyed.

'It was awful,' Roger said.

'Terrible, truly terrible.' Steve shook his head.

'Y'see,' Ethnic began, 'My dad's a big bloke,' Rachel and Peter raised their eyebrows but Ethnic didn't notice. 'He's not easily scared but what happened to him that night, well it broke him.'

'I felt so sorry for him.' Roger shook his head.

'You mustn't blame him Ethnic, what he saw that night would have been too much for anyone.' Steve put a comforting hand on Ethnic's shoulder.'

'What happened? – what did he see?' both girls whispered

as Red rolled her eyes and shook her head.
'Y'see dad got to parents evening early,' Ethnic continued. 'Some of the teachers were already in the hall but not all of them.'
'One of them was missing,' Steve added.
'Yeah which one wasn't there Ethnic?' Roger asked knowing full well the answer.
'Miss Wheeler wasn't there.' Ethnic said sadly, 'so my dad,' Ethnic paused a moment to steady himself, 'my dad went looking for her, he went to her room and - and he just went in he didn't knock –'
'Why would he?' Roger squeaked.
'He couldn't have known.' Steve muttered bitterly.
'I blame myself,' Ethnic's head dropped into his hands. 'I tried to tell him but you know parents.'
'What happened?' the new pupils asked as one, even the youngest of the two girls was growing suspicious now.
'He went into the room and it was dark, so he put the light on and he saw, he saw.' Ethnic raised his head from his hands and leant towards the two youngest, 'He saw her there in her room, hanging upside down from the ceiling!'
'I hate it when she does that,' Steve sympathised.
The new pupils weren't terribly impressed by the boy's tale.
'Look she can be a little volatile,' Red said gently after giving the boys a stern sideways glance.
'Volatile?' Rachel queried suspiciously.

'Yeah, one minute she's fine the next –' Red started.

'The next she's ripping your face off!' Roger cut in.

'The next she's having a go,' Red corrected diplomatically. 'Look most of the teacher's are fine, just watch yourself with Miss Wheeler –'

'Keep some garlic and a crucifix in your pocket.'

Red thumped Roger, 'The thing to remember is that all of the department heads are great, they're all really approachable and if you do have any problems, they'll help.' She finished glaring at the boys.

'So what's the problem with work experience?' Peter asked, directing his question at Red rather than the boys.

'My older brother Russel, well it's Will actually but we all call him Russell for short.' Steve started, answering before Red could. 'Had always wanted to be a vet. When work experience rolled around, Russel asked to be able to spend his week with a local vet. They told him that this wasn't going to happen, as so many students wanted to go into veterinary work every year, it would be impossible to place them all. Therefore veterinary work was not an option for work experience and Russel had to spend his week in the garage of a MOT centre in Cwmbran.'

'Yeah, something similar happened to my mate in our old place.' Mike the shorter of the two boys chipped in.

'Russel however was not easily deterred,' Steve continued proudly, 'He only went and organised his own work experience, a week with a vet in Usk and another week with one in Newport, both in the Summer holidays. But the school refused to consider either as work experience because they hadn't organised it.'

'Yeah I could never figure that, it's only a bit of paperwork surely?' Red added.

'The fact was though that those two weeks did exactly what work experience was supposed to do.' Steve said sitting forward in his equally shabby armchair. 'The vet in Usk was a largely agricultural practice and he loved it, he'd already helped a local farmer with lambing so he easily took the week in his stride. The week in Newport however put him off being a vet for life.'

'Why?' Rachel asked her expression suddenly very serious.

'The first patient was Stripe, a spotted Guinea pig.' Steve began.

'I've got a spotted Guinea pig,' Rachel piped up.

'That's nice,' Steve replied.

'He's called Beckham,' she told him.

'Good with a dead ball, no left foot?'

'He's four,' Rachel added ignoring Ethnic.

'Stripe's owner was an eight year old girl,' Steve tried again. 'She and her mother had brought Stripe in. The girl had bought Stripe some chocolate treats from the pet department of a local garden centre.'

'I know those,' Rachel smiled, 'Beckham loves those.'

'Well um now Stripe had a stone in his bladder the vet told them not to worry an operation would easily fix this but they didn't have pet insurance didn't they? And her Mum couldn't afford £700 for the operation so Stripe had to be put down.' Steve finished.

'What's put down?' Rachel demanded.

'Steve looked to Red (who was slowly shaking her head) for help.'

'It means they kill them with an injection, stone dead in a minute.' Roger got there first.

Rachel's bottom lip started to quiver.

'After this came Barney, an affectionate golden lab and his owner an OAP widower called Sid.' Steve went on in an attempt to get the subject off Guinea pigs, 'Barney was all Stan had, 'You will fix him for me doc' he pleaded. But Barney had a tumour and Stan didn't have pet insurance or fourteen hundred quid.'

'Our Labrador's called Jose.' Rachel said, tears in her eyes now.

Steve stared at her in disbelief, 'So Barney was put down,' he blurted before he could stop himself. 'Y'see a week there and he had a change of heart,' Steve faltered.

'The whole point of Work experience, ' Red dived in before Steve buried himself completely, 'Is to show you whether or not the job is like you thought it would be.' Red said kindly placing her hand on Rachel's shoulder and giving her a tissue, 'A week in that vets lead Russel to a change of heart and he's now in Uni doing something he really loves.'

'Yes,' Steve agreed quickly, 'It all worked out ok in the end, his time in the vet's showed him that it wasn't going to be what he thought it would be.'

'Nope he wanted to help animals not spend the day filling up a skip in the car park with their corpses!' Roger added, getting thumped twice by Red for his trouble.

'This is why work experience is so important, not just box ticking.' Red said firmly.

Ethnic nodded his head. 'My brother Josh (Josh was one of Ethnic's older brothers and like Steve had Aspergers) had considered a career in I.T. He loved computers, especially games and basic programming. The school put him in an office in Blackwood for a week's work experience of I.T. He turned up as instructed at 9pm on Monday morning and was shown to his, completely empty, desk.'

Ethnic paused checking that he'd got everyone's undivided attention. 'Darren, the I.T. manager introduced himself and asked him if he'd brought a book. So Josh says he thought there'd be textbooks there. Then the guy says that he didn't mean textbooks he meant something for him to read as it would be a long day otherwise. Turns out that all Josh had to do in the day was back up the office mainframe at four thirty with a cassette, whole process took six minutes, then he could go home. So Josh asked him what he was supposed to do during the rest of the day and the guy just says that's why I asked if you'd brought a book.'

'By the Wednesday, even with a book, Josh was so bored that he went into the main office and asked if there was anything else he could do there. One of the PA's pointed to a trolley next to the brand new office shredder. She said he could stick the files off the trolley into the shredder, she told him to stick them in one at a time and told him to watch his fingers but she didn't tell him to remove any staples or paperclips first and it didn't occur to Josh, he just did as he was told.' Ethnic finished with a grin.

'And?' Mike asked grinning himself.

'And bang, took out all of the buildings electrics.' Ethnic laughed, 'Stephanie the office manager sent Josh home with a terrible report saying that he clearly had issues! Without saying exactly what she thought Josh's issues were.' Ethnic smirked, 'my mum spent the whole evening persuading my dad not to go into Stephanie's office the following morning, as he wanted to wrap Stephanie's report around Stephanie's head.'

'They're only interested in free labour; my mate went for retail experience in a local shop.' Mike began, 'he spent the whole week moving stock from the old stockroom in the basement to the new stock room on the second floor, no lift he had to carry it all, took him the whole week.'

Everyone in the room tutted and shook their heads.

'He didn't mind, saved him time in the gym he said but the point was, he learnt from one of the girl's there that the new storeroom had been ready for a month but the manager waited until they got someone on work experience in, so she could get them to do all the work for nothing.'

'That's shocking,' Red spat angrily.

'That's not the worst of it,' Mike continued, 'he finished at four everyday and had to go down into the shop to be searched by the manager, in front of a shop full of people before he left, she even made him take his shoes off.'

Red stared back at him open mouthed.

'Didn't you have somebody going round to check up.'

'One teaching assistant for the whole year, none of my lot saw her at all.' Mike replied glumly.

Steve laughed 'They're not all bad my dad did some work for a publisher in Ludlow, the guy he was working for took work experience really seriously. Had each day laid out so that the kids could work through every aspect of the job and get a real idea of what it involved.'

'Yeah that's all fine if you're in Ludlow but here ain't Ludlow.' Roger observed.

'What's that book?' Rachel asked her eyes on the Argonath which Red had open on the table in front of her beside a large OS map.

'This is one of the Argonath volumes that were left to the school a few years back,' Red told her enthusiastically, 'they were left as part of a bequest which – am I boring you? Red asked noticing that Rachel was yawning.

'Can we go now?' Rachel replied to Roger and Ethnic's amusement.

'Yeah, Mr. Dobb's office is left at the end of the corridor; he'll take you to your classes.' Red replied deflated.

'If he's holding a baseball bat when you go in, leg it!' Roger shouted after them as they trooped out of the room. 'So what's all this about, what you up to now?' he added leaning over the map and Red's pile of notes.

Ethnic couldn't help himself, 'We're looking into sightings of a River Troll in the area.'

'It was a Stone Troll,' Roger shouted bristling.

'It was damp and it was green, it was covered in pondweed and it had a net in one hand and a fish in the other, it was obviously and clearly a River Troll.' Steve protested, 'Stone Trolls are blue or –'

'Guy's' Red could see where this was going, 'Roger we've got a medieval map and we're trying to work out where it refers to.' Red handed Roger the photocopy.

Roger studied the map, after about a minute he said, 'But there's no names on it.'

'No Rog that's why it's difficult.'

'But it could be anywhere.'

'No Rog we know it's somewhere in this area.' Red pointed to the large OS map.

'But it's just triangles and circles.'

'Yes I think the triangles are mountains and the circles are ponds and lakes.'

'Why didn't they draw mountains and ponds on the map then so you'd know?'

'Because they didn't.'

'That's dumb.'

'Roger it's a map drawn by a medieval widow.' Steve explained.

'It's still a rubbish map.'

'Roger you like D&D and Adventure fantasy games, maps and treasure. 'Red started.

'Trolls' Ethnic suggested earning a thump from Red.

'But they're done properly; you know mountains that look like mountains and lakes that look like, you know lakes!'

'Well in the real world it doesn't always work like that.' Red told him firmly.

'Why's one mountain got a cross on it?' Roger asked.

Red looked blankly at him for a moment, then pulled the photocopy from his hand, 'what! - where?'

'There look,' Roger pointed to one of three triangles that were grouped together.

The original drawing had been very grainy as it had been copied from a woodcut. On top of that the photocopy itself was pretty grainy so the picture had lots of marks and stains across its surface. As Red looked at where Roger was pointing she could just see that there was indeed a tiny indistinct cross over one of the triangles. The triangle under it, unlike the others, was not formed properly which made it look like the top was broken. Red stared hard at it; something was definitely nagging at the back of her mind. She'd been to Tretower on several occasions and been past it dozens of times, she tried hard to visualise the mountains around the village.

'Triangles can't be mountains then, 'Roger announced, 'there's no mountains round here with crosses on them, must be something else.'

'Such as?' Ethnic asked dryly.

Roger thought for a moment, 'I dunno, maybe Fir trees.'

'Fir trees?' Ethnic and Steve echoed.

'Yeah, Fir trees, Pine trees, like Christmas trees they're a pyramid shape.'

'And the circles?' Steve asked, 'what are they? – Christmas decorations maybe.'

'Or Trolls?' Ethnic added unhelpfully.

Roger left the room, soon followed by Red and the remaining boys as the bell summoned them to their next lessons. The mystery for now would have to wait.

Red lived with her mum about half a mile from the school, her mum worked for the NHS and was currently away on a two month exchange project in Glasgow. This suited Red as relations between them had become quite tense recently; her Mum was under a great deal of pressure at work and didn't cope with it well. The death of Red's dad a few years before and Red's worsening condition added to the stress and made their lives difficult at best. From Red's point of view the Glasgow placement couldn't have come at a better time and she was revelling in her independence. Red joined a neighbour, an OAP called Paul, known to everyone as Bernie, on a shopping trip to the local supermarket.

The arrangement worked well Bernie told her as he had the wheels and she had the nouse! In other words he had the car (with room for a folded wheelchair in the back) and she knew where all the stuff was in the shop. He was good company as well and always insisted on buying her tea and tea cakes in the store's cafe after their shop whilst telling her stories about his national service.
On this occasion his unit had managed to lose control of their Centurion (a tank) as it crossed a farm yard in Germany and skid it sideways through an industrial chicken coup. The consequences, for the chickens at least, were grave and the old farmer, convinced that war had broken out again had then set about Bernie, his mates and the tank with a pitchfork.

Red was giggling over the tale and enjoying her tea cake, when she became aware of a commotion in the corner of the cafe. A rather tall and very plump lady in a striped dress was leading her two granddaughters out of the cafe. As she'd passed the middle-aged waitress she'd stopped to complain loudly. The object of her complaint was the table, or rather the table's occupants, in the corner.

A woman, probably mid forties, sat with her teenage son, the boy clearly had a problem. His left arm and leg were both permanently bent and twisted around at an angle to his body, he kept twisting and turning around in his chair and moaning loudly as his mother tried to feed him his dinner with a fork.

'Shouldn't be brought into a place like this,' the large woman shouted at the waitress,' as her granddaughters craned their necks to watch the boy.

'Got as much right to eat here as you have,' Bernie waded in before the waitress could answer the woman.

'He's not doing you any harm, leave him alone.' A very elderly lady sat on her own at the table beside Red and Bernie contributed with a scowl.

The large lady ignored them both, grimaced at the waitress then swept her grandchildren out of the cafe.

Red's eyes were on the boy's mother, she seemed oblivious to what was going on. She just looked completely and totally defeated, beyond tired, past weary, her eyes were lifeless.

She tidied up the plates as best she could, rose slowly to her feet and gently half led, half lifted the boy, from his chair and began guiding the him out of the cafe. He lurched painfully shuffling from one foot to the other, involuntarily twisting his torso around and back as he did so.

Red grabbed a serviette hoping to conceal the fact that she was crying from Bernie but Bernie didn't miss much.

'Oh love, you mustn't let that upset you,' he reached out for her hand. 'That old trout, shooting off her mouth like that, she'll need help herself one day and that lad and his mother will have . . .'

'That lad killed my best friend.' Red answered quietly.

Bernie stared at Red open-mouthed, the elderly lady on the next table and the waitress both heard her and both produced tissues, handing them to Red. The three of them were now staring at Red and she knew she'd have to explain.

'Not the boys? Nothing's happened to one of them has it?' Bernie asked her in alarm.

'No Bernie,' Red wiped her eyes and blew her nose into the tissue, 'not the boys, they're fine. Her name was Jaz.'

Bernie, the waitress and the elderly lady nodded, all listening intently.

'Jaz was fostered and she kept getting into trouble, she'd been in three schools but she wouldn't fit in. Then they sent her to Millbrook and our headmaster asked Steve and me to keep an eye on her.'

'Take her under your wing like?' The waitress volunteered.

Red nodded, 'I didn't think it was going to work, then I met her and we got on great. It was like she couldn't see the wheelchair we just . . . '

'Just really hit it off?' Bernie contributed.

Red nodded, 'we were all misfits I guess,' then she smiled at a memory,' she was such a laugh, such a wicked sense of humour and she was totally fearless. One of the guys in the year was a real bully and Steve had walloped him so he and his brother jumped Steve on the way home. Jaz saw it happen and waded in, she gave the brother two black eyes and bit off half of his eyebrow.'

'Happy days.' Bernie smiled remembering his own school days.

'Did she do well in school?' The elderly lady asked.

'She was brilliant at chemistry. Old Mr Long loved her to bits, said she took to chemistry like . . .'

'Like a duck to water,' the waitress said.

'How did, I mean what happened, with that lad?' Bernie asked gently nodding towards the table where the boy had been sitting.

Red stared into space composing her words with difficulty, 'I loved Jaz, I could tell her anything and she with me, I never saw her as 'troubled' or difficult she was just Jaz. The Jaz I knew had only one fault . . .'

'She was easily led,' the elderly lady said quietly.

Red turned to the woman, 'Yes exactly, she was easily led.' Red finished what remained of her coffee. 'That boy was Andrew Martin Dawson; I say *was* because the only thing wrong with him when I knew him, when Jaz knew him, was he used to hang out with the wrong people. He'd asked Jaz out and I warned her about him so he backed off but then Mum decided we had to go to see my aunty Jean in France for a fortnight. During the second week Steve was away doing his duke of Edinburgh course.'

'What about that other friend of yours, the one with the mouth?'

'Ethnic's family moved in a month or so after all this happened.'

'So, what happened with the girl?'

'Andrew took Jaz to a party, somebody there took some drugs along, there was something wrong with them, killed Jaz and turned Andrew into what you see today. He only took her to the party cos he was celebrating getting a trial with West Ham.'

'Dear lord two lives ruined and for what?' the waitress said quietly.

'It was three, another kid at the party as well,' Red replied, 'We had police at the school for weeks afterwards. Then the

lectures, then the films but she knew, she knew the harm, knew the danger.' Red could feel herself filling up again, the elderly lady reached over and took her other hand which for some reason helped tremendously. The old lady's deeply lined face had bright blue eyes, she squeezed Red's hand.
'When I found out all I wanted to do was to slap her.' Red told the lady that she'd never seen before.'
'I'd have been the same,' the lady answered firmly.
'Mr Long never recovered, he was so upset by it all, he was past retirement age but he was never going to leave the school, never stop teaching. Then Jaz died and we never saw him again.'
'What a world we live in,' Bernie managed after a moment as the waitress nodded.
The elderly lady kept hold of Red's hand for a few more moments before reluctantly releasing it. Her eyes held Red's a little longer.
Ten minutes later as Bernie and Red rattled across the car park Red found to her surprise that she actually did feel better, maybe talking helped after all.

Four

The Kings Head was a large hotel near both the river and the castle, with a sprawling roundabout separating them. The Major hurried in through the main entrance, glancing at her pocket watch as she did so. She was late and she hated being late.

She knew Newport well although she hadn't been in for a few years, the parking arrangements had changed and the city (a town when she'd last visited) had got a lot busier. She'd eventually managed to park in Baneswell, which was further away from the hotel than she had remembered.

She took the stairs as quickly as her legs would allow and proceeded along a narrow gloomy corridor then into a large exquisitely furnished room with a small bar in the corner.

There were two men in the room, one an elderly waiter carrying a tray bearing a teapot, a small jug and two tea cups and saucers. The other, who was wearing an immaculate three piece suit, rose from his chair with a smile as she entered.

'Malcolm, I'm so sorry the parking,' she began.

'Don't worry yourself,' he said warmly taking her hand, 'I've only just got here myself,'

'I'm in Baneswell.'

'I'm behind the Railway station; all the multi's are full up, the price of progress evidently. It's been a long time.'

'It has, I didn't think I would be able to get you to see me, I couldn't get anywhere with any of your managers.'

'I have a long memory,' Malcolm replied coolly. 'Your work was of great value, the department is in your debt.' He motioned for her to take a seat in one of two armchairs set either side of the small round table that the waiter was stood beside.

'Let me take your coat.' He said easing her raincoat from her shoulders and placing it carefully on a wire coat-hanger suspended from the tall ornate stand in the corner.

'I don't recall the department standing up to be counted when the need arose.'

'Pearls before swine Samantha, you know my views on the subject.' He leant forward picking up his cup from the silver tray that the waiter had placed before them and sitting down opposite the Major. 'For what it's worth you'll always have my ear and for what it's worth *their* priorities have already come back to bite them on the arse.'

Samantha managed a half smile, 'That was always going to be inevitable but I do appreciate the ear.'

'So?'

'Straight to the point Malcolm? - Go on, you know I can't resist. *You* tell me why I'm here.'

The man smiled, took a sip of his tea then carefully returned his cup to its saucer. 'Millbrook.'

The Major smiled, reaching for her own cup, 'Go on.'

'A grinning corpse turns up in the grounds of the very school that houses the Argonath bequest. The corpse has been drained of blood and a former operative involved in the Monmouthshire canal breech cover up, comes knocking on my door. Not too difficult Samantha, and for the record I was going to get in touch with you anyway, though not about this.'

'Go on.'

'Blythefield.'

'Oh you always could pick them; it's all on file, I doubt I could add anything and there's no way that it, or anything like it, could ever happen again.'

Malcolm raised an eyebrow, his expression was unreadable. 'We no longer have the file.'

The Major's expression was clear, 'You've lost the file she said in amazement.'

'Not lost –' he sighed, 'A year or two ago the Cabinet appointed a new and especially obnoxious junior secretary, wanted one of his own staff to have a look at making further efficiencies within the department.'

'A department already cut to the bone by mindless bureaucrats.'

'The young lady in question had legs up to her neck and a brain the size of a walnut. She'd been given unrestricted access so she assumed that gave her access to the restricted files as well.'

'How many?'

'Not many thank God but Blythefield was near the front, all clearly fiction made up by staff with too much time on their hands she said. So she shredded it and a few others as well.'

'Men died.'

'I know Samantha.'

'Where is she now?'

'She's a junior manager at an estate agent's in Wapping I believe.'

'And the junior secretary?'

'Have a guess.'

'Something in Education.'

Malcolm nodded.

'You're not going to ask me to rewrite the whole file from memory are you? Not that it's anything I could ever forget and believe me I've tried.'

'Not today, there's one element of the event that is of interest to me at the moment.'

'Go on.'

'The subjects.'

'What do you want to know?'

'Was there any sign of intelligence, any capacity to think, to plan?'

The Major stared hard into her tea, remembering was clearly unpleasant, 'those in the compound, none whatsoever the door was open, they wanted to get out but couldn't work out how. Three of them were just walking into the walls, not able to step back or turn around. The fourth just lay on the floor screaming. Believe me Malcolm what the soldiers did was a mercy.'

'And they were dead, beyond any doubt?'

'You're going to have to be more specific.'

'Before and after.'

'They were dead before the bullets and they were dead after them.'

'The bodies?'

'The complex was on fire, it was intense and it provided the easiest solution, our brief at the time was containment.'

'What about the one's outside of the complex?'

'There were three, one as mindless as the others, she didn't know where she was or what was happening, another just walked into the fire so I couldn't tell you.'

'And the other?'

'That one got the furthest; it was the youngest subject and the first to have been done. He definitely had a bit more about him, when the soldiers caught him he took the bullets like he was waiting for them, as if he knew it meant release. But if you're asking me if he could think I would have to say that, mercifully, it would only have been at the most rudimentary level.'

Malcolm nodded slowly then reached for his tea, only to draw his hand back sharply as if stung, 'Splinter from yesterday,' he explained, 'didn't feel it at the time.' He sucked the wound for a second, 'feel it now though, who'd plant thorns next to a handrail?' he looked hard at the Major, as if searching her expression for a reaction to his words.

'So Millbrook?' he said after a moment, returning to his tea.

The Major took a deep breath, 'Some of the pupils are involved.'

'You've got minors involved?'

'No Malcolm, *I've* not got minors involved,' the Major spat back angrily, 'they've got themselves involved.' She took a long sip of her tea, 'they're smart kids if I had tried to put them off it would only have made them more determined to continue.'

'How involved?'

'Involved enough to know that there's something extraordinary at the bottom of it all.'

'There is?' Malcolm raised an eyebrow.

The Major stared back hard at him, 'I'm not an idiot Malcolm, or one of your . . . 'she began angrily.

'Samantha you are many things but nobody who knew you would ever call you that, or think of you in that way.' He said calmly, 'But hasn't it occurred to you that you might just know a lot more about this than I do.'

'What about the post mortem?'

'There hasn't been a post mortem yet.'

'What? – Why the hell not?'

'You already know the results of the initial examination and you've seen the press releases, the official and the unofficial. I do admit there's something vaguely unsettling about it all but as far as we're concerned a group of Romanian treasure hunters are over here seeking the Monmouth treasure and they've had a falling out.'

'And the KGB?'

Malcolm leant forward in his chair, 'What?!'

'The KGB,' the Major told him calmly, 'or at least ex KGB if I'm honest.'

Malcolm was clearly not impressed, 'Explain.'

'There are two groups of treasure hunters, the Romanian's and a Russian group, the Russians are ex KGB.'

'I sincerely doubt there's such a thing as *ex* KGB.'

'We searched the house, found letters between the dead man and his sister still in Romania. I've brought you copies.' She pulled a large envelope out of her bag and held it up to him.

'We searched his house? You broke into a crime scene with minors?' Malcolm snapped.

'I did not break into anywhere,' her voice was angry and hurt, 'How dare you Malcolm, how dare you.'

He lifted his hands in apology, 'I'm sorry, look I-'

The Major wouldn't let him finish, 'When the time came to stand up and be counted, you didn't! – How dare you criticize me.'

'I did try but the . . . '
'You did nothing, nothing that counted anyway. What happened to in it together? - What happened to looking after each other? – Come on Malcolm look me in the eye.'
He couldn't.
'The landlord wanted the house back on the market asap; after the police had searched it they released it back to him. I made an appointment for a viewing and took them with me. They found the letter's that everyone else had missed in less than five minutes.' She threw the envelope hard into his lap, 'I've had the letters translated I'm taking them to the police now, I thought that I would give you the copies first as a courtesy, I'm clearly wasting my time.'
She got up from her chair to leave but Malcolm grabbed her wrist, 'Wait, sit back down, please, look if I'm to keep an eye, I'll need their details.'

As it turned out the mystery of the map wasn't going to remain a mystery for long. That same afternoon Red and the boys were making their way along the busy corridor that led to the library. The corridor was crowded with kids; most of the youngsters were wearing school uniform except for a small group wearing tracksuits who were returning from a run.
Steve pulled his phone, which had just beeped out of his pocket. 'Text from the Major look out for any references to

something called the Widows clock?'

Red looked crestfallen, 'There's nothing, there's mention of a Widow's bell but – oh hang on,' Red's smile returned, 'What's Welsh for bell guys?'

Steve grinned to Ethnic who looked blank, 'It's Cloch.'

'That's too close to be a coincidence; it must be the same thing surely.' Ethnic said and Red and Steve nodded. 'Are we getting anywhere with the map?'

Red frowned, 'I've gone through all of our books, there's a couple of references. X is the starting point and the treasure is seven miles from it but we still don't know where X is or in what direction the treasure is from it.'

'So it's another treasure hunt, this time we've got the distance, just not the starting point or the direction?' Ethnic said thoughtfully.

'Yep and this time the clues are six hundred years old' Steve added with a grin.

'Now, there's supposed to be another copy of the map Steve was looking for it on the net.' Red turned to Steve, 'Steven?'

'Yeah I got it, didn't take long at all. 'I left a copy in your locker.' Steve pointed to the long row of Lockers, across the corridor.

'How many times?' Red said exasperated, much to Steve and Ethnic's amusement. 'I don't use my locker.'

Steve jogged over to the lockers and pulled out an A4 sheet from Red's otherwise empty locker. He handed the sheet to

Red, 'I'm not sure it adds anything though.'

Red tugged another sheet from her bag and placed both of them upon her closed laptop which was lying on her lap.

Both maps were broadly similar, at one end three triangles (one with the tiny cross above it) surrounded an X. There were more triangles and a few circles randomly positioned across the map and a single number seven.

The maps were clearly different but both had obviously been copied from the same original.

'Tell you what I did notice though,' Steve said leaning over both maps with Ethnic. 'Look at the end triangle by the X, the one with the broken top. We thought it was a slip of the pen right?'

Red nodded, 'Yes It's the same on yours as well.'

Ethnic suddenly smiled. 'You thought the triangles could be mountains right?' he asked Red.

'Could be and the circles ponds or lakes.'

He looked at Red and Steve with the smuggest grin on his face, 'Oh happy day!'

They'd just reached the school library but Ethnic didn't enter, instead he turned around and raced back down the corridor, leaving Red and Steve bemused as they went in.

In the School library they went to Red's 'desk' beside the computer and printer in the corner. Red opened her laptop and placed it onto the desk. The adjoining table was covered with books including two Argonath volumes.

'So what's this Bell?'

'I think it was part of the Monmouth treasure and I think . . .'

Red was interrupted by Ethnic dragging a third year (Denni) into the library.

'Ta da!' he exclaimed

'What do you want Dalek?'

Red stared blankly back at her.

'You're loser told me you wanted to see me,'

Red looked blank.

'Guy's come on?' Ethnic raised his hands in surprise, like it was the most obvious thing in the world.

Denni aimed a kick at Ethnic which he easily sidestepped, 'Loser!' she shouted at him as she barged past him back out of the Library.

Ethnic grinned at Steve and Red, 'What a delicate little treasure.'

'How's Denni going to help?' they asked him in unison.

'What was Denni wearing?'

Denni was wearing a tracksuit and tee-shirt as she was with a group returning from a run. The tee-shirt she was wearing was light blue with a dark blue logo saying Team Millbrook - Abergavenny three peaks.

'Tracksuit,' they echoed still confused.

'And tee-shirt - same as the one you got right Steve, for that school charity run?'

'Abergavenny three peaks, yeah won't forget that in a hurry.'
Red groaned loudly, causing Ethnic great amusement.
'Oh dear god - I'm an Idiot!' she turned to Steve who was still blank. 'The Blorenge, the Sugar Loaf and the Skirrid. The three mountains surrounding Abergavenny. One of which has a broken top.'
Steve groaned as loudly as Red had and shook his head.
'Aw c'mon! – how could we not - we should have got that.'
'Too right!' she agreed.
'Yeah well I'm not local so for once it isn't my fault!' Ethnic savoured the moment. 'Good job I was here really.'

The town of Abergavenny sat between three mountains and one of them 'Skirrid Fawr' had a massive landslide on its northern tip. Giving the mountain, (a hill in truth) the appearance of having a broken top.
'Don't understand the cross over the broken one though?'Ethnic admitted.
'Oh . . . um well, that'll be cos the locals call it the holy mountain.' Red explained.
'Ethnic was loving this, 'Three triangles, one with a broken top and a cross over it and Aber's got three mountains one with a broken top and called holy! - And neither of you genius' worked it out!'
Steve and Red looked completely embarrassed, Ethnic

slowly shook his head, he knew, that they knew, that he was not going to let them forget this for a long time.

'Ok then why's it called the holy mountain?' Ethic asked after a long pause.

'They say that the landslide on the top was caused by a lightning strike at the moment Jesus was crucified.' Red's eyes returned to the map. 'The mountains aren't quite in the right positions but X *is* Abergavenny, that's the starting point and the treasure is seven miles from it.'

'But in which direction?' Steve wondered.

'Well one good thing came out of all of this.' Ethnic pointed out.

'What?'

'The Major hadn't figured it out either.'

'We've all been trying to tie the map in to Tretower, didn't occur that it could be so close to home.'

Malcolm looked up from his notebook as he finished writing. 'So the girl's in a wheelchair, the one lad's got Aspergers and the other? 'He asked the Major who was just finishing her second cup of tea.

'Jamel, they call him Ethnic.'

'Well you were always a one for diversity.' The Major said dryly. 'You're sure that there's something there?'

'Yes positive, Jenifer was right, at the time that Argonath was collating accounts, there was nothing in nature to suggest that amphibians could possess such qualities. And I assume you read the file.'

'The canal breech, yes of course, recommended reading now. There's no chance your creature was part of all that?'

'No, it reacted to the flood rather than being part of the cause. Jane was just part of the follow-up and talked to the copper. There was clearly a story there but it was a different story.'

'I saw her notes, she wanted time for you and she to make a proper examination, the proposal she submitted was sound enough and nobody could question her judgement but-'

'Cutbacks.'

Malcolm nodded, 'did you see her proposal?'

'No but I knew what was in it. We had a researcher at the time, lovely, lovely girl, Jeanette she was really sharp, went back through the press, found all the accounts. Once you saw the list there was no doubting that there had to be something behind it all.'

'One thing did puzzle me though, her proposal is still on file, do you know what name she gave it?'

The Major shook her head.

'The Widows clock, bit of a strange name for an investigation proposal don't you think?' he asked studying her face as he spoke.

'Yes very odd.' The Major kept her expression blank.

Malcolm finished his tea and rose from his chair, 'I'll just go and settle up.'

'Let me-'

'Wouldn't dream of it,' he told her with a smile and headed towards the bar pulling his wallet from his pocket.'

Whilst his back was turned the Major surreptitiously slipped her phone from her pocket and quickly typed out a short text message, she pressed send and slipped her phone back into her pocket before Malcolm had turned back around and returned to the table.

'You must miss her.' he said quietly.

'Jane? - terribly' the Major whispered back, then with a flash of anger, 'A parachute jump at her age, what was she thinking?' she snapped. 'Stupid, stupid girl why, why did she do it?' She finished looking more hurt than angry.

'She did it because that was her,' Malcolm smiled warmly leaning forward to take the Majors hand. 'She was never going to quietly accept retirement, rather like somebody else I can think of.'

The Major smiled in spite of herself.

'Malcolm what I said to you was cruel and unwarranted.'

'Not entirely unwarranted.'

'It's just these kids, I would like you to meet them, they don't disappoint, I really like these kids.'

Malcolm grinned, 'I can see that, is this, the long buried maternal streak finally coming through?'

'They're good kids.'
'Take the letters to the police; let's get all the foreign nationals rounded up. If there are ex KGB amongst them, that will complicate matters and they'll take some finding so don't hold your breath. I'll get in touch when they're out of the picture, I'll share anything with you that they tell the police. We'll let the dust settle, then perhaps we'll have a look. As for now,' he folded the list and put it into his jacket pocket. 'You have my word that we'll keep an eye.'
'Good enough,' the Major stood up and shook his hand.

The following Thursday was a particularly busy Thursday so Red had got into school early as she knew she wasn't going to have much free time. Steve and Ethnic were in early as well. A sponsored cross country run had been organised with Monmouth comp, to raise money for Jones four whose broken leg had become infected following his time in the river.
They saw Harold Williams who was shouting into his mobile but paused to give them a cheery wave before resuming his rant. They had just passed the open door of a classroom when Red had an overwhelming feeling that something was wrong. She stopped her chair and looked around them, then without really knowing why, she turned her chair into the classroom. For a moment everything seemed fine then she saw her. Miss Tanner one of the newly

qualified teachers was on the floor beside her desk, she was completely motionless, her skin unnaturally pale, she looked dead.

Red screamed.

The effect was instant, Ethnic and Steve had carried on up the corridor both distracted by Bomb-man five on Steve's phone. Neither had noticed that Red had stopped and turned into the classroom. Harold Williams was still ranting with the builder who was supposed to be in re-pointing the wall at the back of the car park. The second they heard Red's scream however the three of them bolted for the classroom, crashing through the door at such a speed that they nearly took the classroom door off its hinges.

In a second Harold and Ethnic were kneeling beside the fallen teacher and Steve was calling an ambulance.

'I can't, I can't feel a pulse.' Harold gasped holding her wrist and 'She' so cold.' He was normally the personification of calm unflappability, he wasn't now.

Whatever had happened had caused her to drop her handbag the contents of which were scattered across the floor around her. Ethnic picked up a small makeup mirror and held it in front of her mouth.

'She's breathing look,' he said quietly.

'Thank God,' Harold noticeably calmed, 'yes, yes there *is* a pulse, very faint.'

Red pointed, 'Look at her other hand,' Harold was holding her right hand and she was partially lying on her left. Red could see that her left hand was badly swollen and discoloured.
Harold and Ethnic gently rolled her onto her back to get a better look at the hand, whilst Steve was describing what had happened to Ambulance control.
'There's an Ambulance on its way, is there any medication or medical cards or hospital letters in her bag.' Steve shouted.
Ethnic checked the bag and quickly sorted through the objects on the floor, 'No – nothing.'
'Steve go outside and wait for the ambulance so you can bring them straight here.' Harold was still clearly anxious. 'She's so cold.'
Red pulled her coat from the back of the chair and threw it over to Harold and Ethnic.
Barely five minutes after Steve had rung; he was running back into the class room with another Steve and his colleague Mark, the Ambulance crew. They had the unconscious young teacher on a stretcher in moments and soon whisked her away with Harold going with them.
By any standards it had been a bizarre start to the day but it was about to get even more so.
Barely half an hour later Red's first lesson was interrupted by Mr Powell one of the biology teachers, who stuck his

head around the door and barked, 'I need Jenifer now!' much to the rest of the classes amusement.

Once outside as well as Mr Powell she found Ethnic and Steve (whose run had been cancelled) and Mr Dobbs the head of Biology. The two teachers hurried off along the corridor without an explanation and with Red and the boys in pursuit. They soon reached the block where they'd found the unfortunate teacher. That classroom like all the others adjoining it had obviously been emptied.

'We've cleared the block,' Mr Powell told them as they went into the classroom. This wasn't entirely true as Mrs Dean another young teacher and friend of Miss Tanner was picking up the handbags contents which were still all over the floor.

Mr Dobbs turned to face Red and the boys, his face a picture of concern. 'Harold's rung, they're sure she's been bitten by a snake.' He gasped, trying to get his breath back from racing through the corridors. 'Did you see any movement when you entered the room? Anything?' he asked Red looking desperate. 'The hospital needs to know what kind of snake it was.'

'Snake bite! You're joking right?'

'Jamel do I look like i'm joking?'

He didn't.

'Well it's got to be an Adder surely?' Red flustered, 'Snake bite are they sure?'

'No Jenifer, Adder's are pretty straight-forward, effects and treatment.' Mr Powell told her firmly.

'Well it's something from the school or maybe she's reacting to the bite, like she's allergic maybe?' Red replied.

Mr Powell sighed, 'No Jenifer, this is venom from a bite; we have two corn snakes, not poisonous, both accounted for and on the other side of the school. Did you see anything when you came in the room?'

'Get that container,' Steve pointed to the small plastic container that the teachers had brought into the room.

'What? – why?' My Dobbs asked (but he was picking up the container as he did).

'Because she was on the floor beside her desk and chair when we found her, like she'd been sat at her desk when it happened.'

'Yes but I don't understand,' Mr Dobbs said following Steve who was walking determinedly towards her desk'

'It's one of the new style teacher's desks isn't,' Steve said.

'Oh God' Red and Ethnic both realised what Steve was thinking. 'With the draws that close automatically,' Red moaned.

Steve grinned at Mr Powell, 'Bet you didn't think to look in the draw did you.' Mr Powell went white.

Steve reached for the draw handle.

'No let me,' Mr Powell eased himself in front of Steve and carefully opened the draw whilst Mr Dobbs opened the plastic container.

'Is it there?' Ethnic asked as he grabbed and brandished a hockey stick in the corner of the room.

In answer Mr Powell reached in and grabbed a small nondescript snake which he carefully lifted from the draw. Holding it firmly behind the head he dropped it into the case as Mr Dobbs clipped the lid back on.

The case was put on the tabletop and everyone peered in at the unassuming foot long snake. 'This is a disaster Mr Dobbs breathed, it could be anything, it's not British but if we don't know where it's from it'll take hours to identify it.'

The snake was basically brown with a greenish tinge at the tail, with a few faint partial bands of a slightly darker colour along its back. Steve took a photograph with his phone then dragged the picture into an image search box. He held up his phone which was now covered in pictures of similar looking snakes all with different names, 'Going to need a country of origin.' He announced gravely.

'But how did it get here?' Mrs Dean mumbled.

'Look,' Mr Dobbs took charge, we'll get this down to the hospital, you three (he looked at Red and the boys) if you can find out anything,' he pulled a card from his pocket and gave it to Steve, 'That's my mobile.' They raced out of the room with the snake.

Red turned to Mrs Dean, 'You share this room with Miss Tanner right? Miss Dean said that she did.

'Had Miss Tanner fallen out with any of the kids? Or have you seen any of them on their own in here recently?'

Mrs Dean thought for a moment, then her face brightened 'That Jones boy, third year, he was in here last night when I came to get my bag, said he was looking for his calculator.'

'Which Jones?' Steve and Ethnic asked together.

'Tall, thin, wiry hair, looks like someone's taken a bite out of one of his ears.

Ethnic and Steve looked at each other, 'Jones nine' they said in unison. 'Where will he be now?'

'Upper music room, Miss Jenkins.' Mrs Dean was already racing out of the room followed by Red and the boys.

They reached the upper music room in barely a minute, Red was thankful she was in her powered chair as she wouldn't have been able to keep up otherwise.

Mrs Dean reached for the door but Steve and Ethnic stopped her.

'Let us to this,' Steve said quietly, 'There's only so much you can do and it'll take time. Me and Steve will have the information in seconds.'

'Trust them, they will.' Red told her earnestly.

'Mrs Dean looked both boys in the eyes, 'Don't kill anyone.'

'Get Miss Jenkins out of the way.'

Miss Dean stuck her head round the door and called Miss Jenkins out as Steve and Ethnic went in.

The room was spacious and well lit because one wall had large continuous windows running its full length. The windows overlooked the school water feature. The water feature ran parallel to, and the length of, the back of the school. It was a concrete channel filled with cobbles and a foot of water. It was about three feet wide for most of its length, widening to a large square pool beneath the raised music suite. When it was completed it looked really effective, marginal plants and bog plants were added at various points and even some dwarf lilies. It didn't take long for the algae and blanketweed to take hold however and soon the ground staff were locked in a never ending annual battle with the algae and weed to keep the feature looking half decent.

Steve walked straight up to Jones nine, 'Where did you get the snake? He spat.

Jones nine answered with two words the second of which was off, Steve leaned over grabbing him by the scruff of the neck and hoisted him out of his chair.

'He's not going to tell you anything.' Maddock the largest of the third year boys told him. We don't dob each other in do we?'

'We don't have time for this,' Steve told Ethnic, 'there's only one way I can convince them how serious this is.' He let go of Jones and walked over to Maddock.

Maddock was the biggest boy in the class and a known bully; as soon as Steve approached him he leapt up, swinging a punch at Steve. Steve grabbed his fist with his hand and squeezed hard, Maddock dropped to his knees with a yelp, Steve keeping hold of his fist, grabbed the back of his belt with his free hand and lifted him bodily off the floor.

Ethnic was struggling to keep a straight face, 'Don't attempt to land on your feet son, from this height you'll break both ankles. Try and land flat, even though the waters shallow it should break your fall, probably well maybe.'

Steve marched towards the windows carrying the boy, 'Right Maddock, pick a window.'

'Adams tell him, tell him now!' Maddock shrieked.

Steve dropped Maddock to the floor, he and Ethnic turned to Adams who was sat at a desk in the opposite corner. They grabbed him firmly, dragged him from his desk and frog-marched him out of the room.

In the corridor Red and the two teachers were waiting, Steve and Ethnic pushed Adams up against the wall staying either side of him, the two glaring teachers stood directly in front of him.

'Where did you get the snake?' Mrs Dean hissed furiously.

Steve and Ethnic couldn't imagine Mrs Dean throwing her weight around, she was only a few inches over five feet and painfully thin. Now however, she was bristling and seemed ready to explode in an instant. Ethnic and Steve were impressed.

It was all too much for Adams. 'It was a Slow Worm,' he blurted. 'I found it and showed it to Jones nine and he wanted it to-'

'Where did you find it?' Both of the teachers demanded in unison.

'Garden centre across the road, me, Jones nine and Williams thirteen were in early for detention, my brother works in the garden centre and he was unloading some large pots off a lorry. I went to give him a hand and it was in the bottom of one of the pots so I put it in my pocket.'

'Where was the delivery from? What country?' The teachers demanded.

'I dunno, it was only a Slow-'

Steve and Ethnic were already racing down the corridor and out of the school. They knew the garden centre well as they'd both worked there collecting trolleys during the summer holidays and carrying trees to cars at Christmas. They ran across the road and into the car park. To their immense relief they found most of the shrub department boys were all outside surrounding the forklift which wouldn't start.

'If you're trying to escape it's no good hiding here, they'll soon find you.' One of them shouted.
'Guys delivery yesterday morning, ceramic pots, Adams and his brother were unloading; there was a snake in one of them which bit one of the teachers, where did the pots come from?' Steve panted.
'You're having a . . . ' The two nearest guys Ken and Jeff had worked with Ethnic and Steve many times and assumed at first that this was another wind up but they all soon realised it wasn't. 'What? Are you serious?'
'Thailand.' One of the managers said firmly, 'let me double check.' He raced off towards the shrub-hut.
Steve handed Ethnic the card with Mr Dobbs' phone number, then quickly started typing into his own phone whist Ethnic pulled his phone from his pocket.
'Adams thought it was a Slow-worm,' Ethnic explained as he typed the number into his phone. 'Took it to show his mates and one of them thought it would be hysterical to put it in one of the teachers draws.' Ethnic explained to the guys.
'Bloody hell, was that what that ambulance earlier was?'
Ethnic and Steve nodded as Colin stepped of the hut, holding a large Blue file. 'Pattaya, Thailand.' He shouted.
Ethnic was already ringing Mr Dobbs as Steve stabbed a finger onto the screen of his phone, 'Got it! – Ethnic?' he turned the phone to Ethnic, who peered at the image then nodded and gave him a thumbs up.

'That's the bugger.'

Ethnic handed his phone to Steve.

'Mr Dobbs the snake came from the garden centre opposite; it arrived on a truck yesterday morning from Pattaya in Thailand, we think its Callo- Callio-.' Steve struggled with the Latin name.

'Calliophis maculiceps' all of the shrub boy's readout aloud over Steve's shoulder.

'You beauties' Mr Dobbs shouted loud enough for everyone to hear then hung up.

'Good job you know your Latin.' Ethnic told the boys with a sigh of relief.

'Working with plants kid.'

Colin returned to the group as Dave two, Wayne, Paul, Malcolm, Justin and Ben joined it. The forklift forgotten, now that stowaway poisonous snakes were the issue.

'Here do you reckon there'll be any more of them?'

'We better check, though I doubt they'll have survived the night here.'

'Not if it was outside.'

'No there was a bit of a frost last night.'

'Here remember that scorpion that came in with those cacti.'

'Yeah massive black thing.'

'Claws like pliers.'

'No that Scorpion didn't survive.'

'No but that was cos Dave from aquatics sat on it.'

'Aye, fastest I've ever seen him move.'

'Yeah, we'd better get back; we'll let you know what happens.' Steve and Ethnic left them with a wave.

Five

Although they didn't know it at the time the events of the morning would have repercussions which would result in Red finally getting hold of the information that she'd been looking for.

Firstly the young teacher would go on to make a full recovery; she was kept in hospital for observation for a couple of days but there was no lasting damage.

Secondly Mr Dobbs tracked them down later that afternoon in the Library. He thanked them profusely then asked if they liked their food. To Steve and Ethnic this was a no-brainer so they agreed to whatever he had in mind before they even knew what it was.

It turned out to be a meal out at a local pub called Foxhunter (named after the horse)'Did they know it?' he asked.

They did indeed, Steve and Red had both gone in there with family and more recently Ethnic had gone in to get directions when they were trying to find the Majors cottage (which was a little further along the same lane).

Red and the boys turned up the following Sunday evening, and found not only Mr Dobbs, his wife Penny and his younger sister Juliet. In addition Harold Williams was there with his wife Gloria and Robert James who was Miss Tanner's fiancé.

The evening went well, the kid's didn't have to pay for anything and there was so much food that even Steve and Ethnic had to eventually admit defeat. Harold Williams and Mr Dobbs (another Steven they discovered) were completely different outside of school, Mr Dobbs in particular; it turned out, had a wicked sense of humour and frequently had the whole table helpless with laughter. Robert James spent his time repeatedly thanking everyone and buying rounds of drinks, which meant copious amounts of lemonade for the youngsters and two very merry senior teachers by the end of the session.

Towards the end of the meal the conversation turned to sport and what Swansea needed to ensure premiership survival. It was at this point that Juliet (who'd been the quietest during the evening) came and sat next to Red.

'So Jenifer, Steven tells me that you've been working your way through the Argonath volumes.'

Red nearly spilled her drink; Juliet was blonde and very pretty and didn't look the type to have even heard of Argonath.

'Yes, well at least trying to work my way through them' she replied with enthusiasm.

'You're so lucky the bequest was after my time.'

'You went to Millbrook?'

'Yes and I had, well still have if I'm honest, a fascination with cryptozoology.'

'I'm not sure you look the type,' Red laughed.

'I'm not sure if that's a compliment,' she giggled back. 'I love all of that sort of stuff. I heard about Argonath through Baker (Baker was a modern historian who'd catalogued Argonath amongst others). At the time I had a real bee in my bonnet about Teggie.

Red hadn't been sure what to make of Juliet at first but the woman had one of the most amazing smiles she'd ever seen, it lit up her whole face. Within barely a minute Red felt like she'd known her for years and could trust her with anything.

'Yes that's Bala Lake isn't it?' Red replied enthusiastically, 'The Nessie of Wales, have you ever been to Bala?'

Juliet laughed out loud, 'Been there? – Sweetheart I practically moved in. Spent a fortnight of my holidays before Uni camped out at the lake hunting the thing.'

'Did you see anything?'

'Of the creature, No.' She shook her head sadly, 'Of Kevin Kendall rather too much.' She replied with a flash of smile.

'Kevin Kendall?'

'Founder of the MCZS, that's Millbrook Crypto Zoological society before you ask.'

'You had a society?'

'There were five of us,' Juliet laughed, 'and we had a Camper van and a dog.'

'Oh please tell me you called the dog-.'

She shook her head, 'Barney- yeah we missed a trick there.'

Red was laughing now, 'So you went to Bala to see the monster.'
'We went to Bala to *catch* the monster, on film anyway.' She drew her head closer to Red's and lowered her voice, 'So it's midnight and I'm sat with an old Zenith and a flashgun in a reed-bed waiting for the creature to surface.'
'Sounds good so far,' Red giggled, 'why do I get the feeling that this story doesn't end with the greatest scientific discovery of modern times.'
'It would almost certainly have resulted in the greatest scientific discovery of modern times if Kevin Kendall hadn't climbed into the bulrushes with me. I thought he was coming in to help.'
'I think I know where this is going now.' Red managed between giggles.
'It soon became obvious what was really on his mind so I pushed him into the lake and then I had to dive in and get him out cos he couldn't swim.'
The two girls collapsed into a fit of laughter just as Harold's wife Gloria, a very large and very jolly lady, concluded an impassioned speech on the need for Paul Clements to get the team playing the way that they used to and play to their strengths. 'No need to over-complicate, just get crosses into the box, you've got Llorente who's lethal in the air and if he's not in a scoring position he can just nod it down to Sigurdsson who'll bury it. It's a no-brainer.' She told the

table.

Red and Juliet eventually regained their composure around about the time that the conversation on the rest of the table turned to county (Newport County).

'Okay then what was your theory?' Red asked once she'd got her breath back.

'There's Gwyniad in the lake, a fish that dates back to ancient times and they're only found in Lake Bala.' Juliet began thoughtfully. 'So if there's one relic population in there-'

'There might be another.'

'Yeah, I know it's a long shot but who knows.' She finished her wine and Robert appeared instantly with a bottle. 'No thanks Robert I've had more than – okay thanks, yep that's lovely thanks,' Juliet picked up the now full glass and winked at Red, 'Good job I'm not driving tonight.'

Roger hovered over Red, 'Please let me get you another.'

'Roger I'm fine honestly.' Red wasn't sure how disabled friendly the toilets were so she didn't want to drink too much but Roger had other ideas.

'I'd just like to say again,' he said lowering a lemonade and lime onto the table in front of her, 'how grateful Caroline and I are, if you hadn't found her –'his voice tailed off. He was a very earnest young man Red decided and the young teacher clearly meant a great deal to him. 'If you hadn't found her –'

'Roger we all did what anyone would do, she's a super teacher and we're all really especially fond of her.' Red lied, having never been in a class with her, nor spoken to her.

Roger staggered back to his chair and Mrs William's assessment of the current off-side rule.

Red turned back to Juliet, 'Wasn't there something about a secret military experiment?'

Juliet nodded enthusiastically, 'Yes, blimey girl you're well informed.' Red could see the wine was beginning to get to Juliet now, her cheeks were getting rosier by the minute and there was a slight slur to her speech. 'The story was that in the run up to war the army decided to train a small number of Seals to swim up to boats and place magnetic mines on their hulls under the water.'

Juliet paused for another sip,' they took the Seals and a trainer to Bala and started to practice with a few smaller boats on the lake. The idea was sound enough, Seal's are smart enough to be trained and once the Seal reached the boat the magnet would take over.'

'Did it work?'

'Bloody disaster!' Juliet shook her head, 'According to one of the locals all they managed to do was set fire to the boat shed and blow up a Swan.'

Both girls collapsed into another fit of giggles.

'So, go on then,' Juliet nudged Red finally, 'what are you looking into?'

'I am getting nowhere fast, I'm looking into Gregory of Caldicot,' Red started.

Juliet's face lit up, 'Ah the Widows Bell.'

Red couldn't believe her ears. 'What? – how do you know about that?'

Juliet smiled, 'Have you ever heard of the PRB?'

Red looked blank.

'The Pre-Raphaelite Brotherhood.'

'The painters? – sorry yes, group of Victorian painters.' Red thought for a moment, 'Millais, Hunt and –'

'Rossetti,' Juliet finished for her. 'They founded the movement yes and there were poets, designers and architects as well as painters.'

'Okay, so how do they fit in?'

Juliet finished her drink as Roger put another full glass of white wine in front of her and this time a coke in front of Red. 'Dante Gabriel Rossetti had a sister, also a poet.'

Red smiled, 'Yes Christina, she wrote the Goblin Market.'

'Yes she did and Christina had a friend called Vivian, Vivian Bennett.'

'You've got to stop,' Red held her hand up and reached for her backpack on the back of the chair. She pulled out a battered notebook and fished round for a pen. A moment later she was furiously scribbling notes as Juliet told her the story.

'Vivian was a model for Waterhouse and Arthur Hughes. The Pre-Raphaelites loved myths and legends and Vivian had welsh ancestry. She'd seen the original welsh poem called the Widow's bell, which is now lost before you ask, and she wrote a contemporary account of it.' Juliet slowed down to give Red enough time to write it all down. 'The poem is pretty much a commentary on the Brecon window.'

'The Brecon window?' Red looked up her face blank.

Juliet laughed, 'Argonath clearly hadn't got all the facts then, mind you I suppose this was after his time. There was a chapel outside Brecon which was destroyed by lightening in the 1850's. The stained glass window was salvaged because it was so unusual and eventually it fell into the hands of William Morris. Vivian realised that the poem and the window were depicting the same event.'

Red stared at Juliet completely fascinated, 'Please, please tell me that pictures of the windows or copies of the poem remain.'

Juliet's face broke into another huge smile, 'I've got copies of both and I'm going past your school tomorrow. I'll drop them off at the library for you if you like.'

'If you could that would be wonderful thanks. Tell me about the poem.'

'Think of the pied piper but with a monster instead of rats. The bell was also called rattle and flute by Vivian and it was some kind of devise that enabled it's user to call up and control a monster.'

'Call it up?'

'Yeah the monster slept under a hill beside a lake. The widow climbed the hill under a full moon and she could summon it and control it, a bit like the Gollum legend I suppose.'

'I'd like to propose a t-toast,' Roger was on his feet now, glass held high in the air, swaying like a tree in a gale. 'On behalf of Caroline and – and-' he had to stop and think for a moment.

'Oh dear god,' Red said under her breath causing Juliet to collapse into giggles again.

'And myself, I'd like to propose a toast to all of you and especially to – to' he pointed to Red his face blank.

'To Jenifer,' Mr Dobbs and Harold Williams climbed wobbling to their feet beside him.

'To Jenifer,' everyone at the table echoed. Red sank into her seat blushing and silently promising retribution on Steve and Ethnic who were grinning hugely at her discomfort.

'And furthermore-'Roger started before losing his balance and falling backwards over his chair sending both the chair and himself crashing onto the wooden floor. Mr Dobbs and Harold attempted to get him back on his feet.

'Juliet, who's driving?' Red whispered in alarm.

'Penny's been on mineral water all evening, so she's taking Steve and I. Harold and Gloria are taking a Taxi. Roger did drive here but Harold took his keys off him earlier. He'll be on someone's settee tonight then he can pick up his car sometime tomorrow.'

Juliet was as good as her word; Red went into the Library the following lunchtime to find a large battered box file had been dropped off for her. Red pulled it open to find pages and pages of handwritten notes and a neat A4 drawing.
Red had hoped to see Juliet again as she had so enjoyed the young woman's company and humour and she was sorry she'd missed her. But there was a note with her phone number and email address, so she'd at least be able to get in touch and thank her again.
Red spent the whole of the afternoon working carefully through the notes (missing a lesson in the process). By the time Ethnic and Steve found her at the end of the afternoon, all the random pieces of the puzzle that she'd wrestled with over the last few weeks were beginning to slot together and form a larger, clearer picture.
'Major wants a meet,' Steve said holding up his phone. 'I've told her about the map,' he added grinning at Ethnic.
'She swore,' Ethnic told Red beaming happily.
'Okay well Juliet came up trumps; it's all starting to fit together now.' She told them, 'Services?'

Both boys nodded.

Raglan services were two identical buildings sitting on either side of the A449, the dual carriageway running from Newport through to Monmouth and the Midlands. They were both new buildings which had replaced the old service station. Red and the boys had been here on numerous occasions, from Red's point of view there was plenty of room and everything was well laid out and level. The boys dived into Greggs whilst Red rattled towards Subway.

When the Major arrived five minutes later she found the three of them surrounding a small round table which was buried under food packaging. The Major got herself a cup of tea whilst Red made the boys make space for her on the table.

The eating area was spacious with a few tables surrounded by low soft armchairs. Each table and chairs had a lot of room between it and the next one. It was an ideal place to meet and talk as nobody else was able to eavesdrop.

The Major was soon sat with them tea in hand, 'Most of the papers are letters from Nicolae's sister Christina.' She began. 'We've waded through all of them and I think we can piece together his side of the story. He was in this country on a search. He'd found something in a small provincial Russian museum, a misidentified item that convinced him that the treasure of Monmouth was real and still hidden. He'd tried to buy it from them as it was only a minor exhibit but they wouldn't sell. So he got a local clock-maker to build a replica based on photographs then he bribed a guard to allow him to swap the two items.' The Major paused to sip her tea, 'He put together a team and they travelled over last year. The intention had been to arrive later this year but with all the rumours surrounding the Brexit referendum they came earlier. It's obvious that they hadn't got the final destination of the treasure just the starting point and the distance from the starting point.'

Red and the boys exchanged glances, they were huddled together around the Major who was speaking really quietly, despite the fact (as with the Garden centre) that nobody was in earshot.

'Somebody in Russia knew more but wanted a share of the treasure, Christina was negotiating with them and trying to work out the location from papers over there.' The Major continued furtively, 'Not long after this, Christina wrote to warn Nicolae that she'd discovered the man she'd been negotiating with was ex KGB and that he'd left Russia with another group before Christmas, presumably to come here and search for themselves.

'KGB!?'Ethnic blurted through his coke.

The Major raised an eyebrow in Ethnic's direction, then continued. 'It's difficult to be sure as we've had to try and work out what Nicolae's written to Christina by using her reply to him. But it's clear from her last letter that something had happened. He told her that they were near to the end of their task and that he would return with not just the treasure of Monmouth. He'd discovered a second treasure but he needed the first treasure to unlock it.'

'What did he mean a second treasure?' Red gasped.

'So there's two groups of Russians over here looking for it, one of which is KGB?'

The Major continued calmly sipping her tea, 'Russians and Romanians, yes. Christina wrote to Nicolae to warn him but he wasn't worried, he told her that without the clock anyone who made any attempt to recover the treasure was doomed. They had also worked out that the starting point was Abergavenny but they didn't know either in which direction the treasure lay. So they literally drew a circle around Abergavenny on the map. That's their first mistake. They're all working their way around it; getting themselves employment as farm-workers, labourers, ground workers any jobs going in the area. Anything to get them outside and able to search but it's a huge area and so far none of them have found a thing.'

'How do you know that?' Steve asked.

'Because they're still here and if they're still here they're still looking.'

'You said first mistake?' Red finished her lemonade and gathered up the remains of the food packaging.

The Major smiled, 'The map was drawn by a medieval widow, she had no means to make accurate measurements. Today we think of maps looking down, a bird's eye view, that's a modern concept. She'd drawn the map more as a set of instructions that her son would have understood and followed on the ground. On her map the placement of the mountains around Abergavenny is drawn as you'd see them from a specific point on the ground rather than an accurate plan view.'

Red passed the packaging to Ethnic and pointed to the bin which he was the nearest to.

'Um this is all very interesting but can we go back to the bit about a gang of KGB killers wandering around the countryside. Major don't you think . . .' Steve cut in.

'That it's time to call the police. Yes, I'm sorry I had no choice.' The Major agreed. 'One man is dead and there's two groups out there searching the same area for the same thing. I had to but I've not told them the whole story, frankly because I don't know it myself and what I do know, they wouldn't believe. I've told them that the victim was a member of a group of treasure hunters and that there is a rival group also searching the area for the treasure of Monmouth. They have some names and they'll find the rest, then they'll round them up but of course we know there's a lot more to this story.'

The Major finished her tea as Ethnic binned the remains of the rubbish. 'Now my dear, please, please tell me that you've found something out about the Widows clock, I've got nowhere.'

'The widows clock, no nothing.'

The Major looked crestfallen.

'But that's because it's not called the Widows clock, it's the Widows Bell, the Welsh for Bell is cloch we think it got miss-translated.

The Major rolled her eyes and shook her head, 'Oh of course it is, I didn't think of that, what have you got?'

Red put on a black framed pair of reading glasses and pulled a notebook from her bag. 'The Widows Bell, also called rattle or flute, is in the first Argonath and it's the subject of an ancient Welsh poem. The poem was translated by a Victorian named Vivian Bennett.' Red began. 'Vivian was a friend and contemporary of Christina Rossetti. She'd

seen the original welsh poem, which is now lost and wrote a contemporary account of it. You ready for this?'
'Brace yourself,' Ethnic grinned.
'I've taken the account from the Argonath volume one and put it with Vivian's and this is what you get. There was a maiden of great beauty from either Tretower or Crickhowel depending on which account you read but these towns are close to each other so I doubt that matters. One night she's rushing home through a terrible storm and she sees a strange shining chariot fall from the sky. There were two aboard, one in the likeness of man but of glass and metal, his body all interlocking rods and wheels which were broken and smashed by the fall. The other was a man tall and strong with the face of an angel, he was badly hurt and speaking gibberish. She went for help, the villagers were not afraid of him and they carried him back to the village where he was nursed by the maiden. As time went on he recovered quickly and was liked by everyone who met him. He and the maiden fell in love married and had a son. He learnt the villager's language and taught them many things. He also made things, wonderful devices the like of which had never been seen before. He took the remains of his chariot and used them to fashion seven wonders, seven gifts for his wife and her people.'
Red paused whilst a small group of walkers passed close to their table, once they had gone she continued.
'Each of these gifts enabled the villagers to improve and control different aspects of their lives. One greatly improved the way that they worked the land, increasing the yield of their crops and boosting the harvest. Another allowed them

to tame animals that were previously uncontrollable. One healed all wounds and sickness and another was a weapon that would destroy any living thing that it touched. The gifts empowered the people and enabled them to thrive in a difficult unforgiving world. The villagers called him Seren and they loved him. Then exactly a year after he'd arrived a traveller brought sickness to the village. The Argonath says that Seren used something he called dagrau angylion to make up a potion that cured them however he only had time to make up a small amount and many were sick. His wife made sure that everyone got some but there was only enough left for one final dose. He told her the sickness would not affect him so she took it and he died the following day.'

The Major looked in amazement from Red to the boys, 'She hasn't finished yet, wait til you here the next bit.' Ethnic told her enthusiastically.

'Word of the wonders that had been done soon got around and all the local markets marvelled at the size and quality of the goods and produce from the village. But then talk of witchcraft and black magic began so the widow took the devices, the treasure and hid them far away from the village. Only one item (called Cloch) she kept back burying it in a wood near the village.' Red continued. 'The following year a Nobleman came into the village and demanded to see what the stranger had made. The Nobleman threatened the widow's child. The widow realised that he didn't know how many devices had been made, so told him that there had only been one and that it had stopped working when her husband had died. She took him to where the Bell was buried and swore on the child's life that the bell was all she had. He gave her son back to her but took the bell for himself. The nobleman was called; Red paused raising her eyes from her notes to the Majors, 'Raven.'

'The treasure of Monmouth,' the Major whispered.

'Now the widow intended that her son would be given the treasure when he came of age for this was his birthright. Thirteen years later however she fell in love with another man, she begged him to steal the Bell back from Raven, telling him that with it she had the means to summon and control a deadly guardian who would keep them safe and open the path to the treasure. This second lover isn't named but I'll bet you anything it's –'

'Gregory of Caldicot.' The Major's face was a picture; the boys couldn't stop themselves from giggling.

Red pressed on, hitting her stride now. 'Vivian saw a drawing of the Bell and described it as like a large Egg, like that of a Swan or a Goose. It was silver and inscribed with waves and stars and out of both ends was a mouth piece like that of a flute. She also had a drawing copied from a stained glass window from a chapel outside Brecon. (Red handed the Major the A4 sheet that Juliet had given her) That's the drawing, the chapel's long gone I'm afraid.'

The drawing had three panels, in the first, a young woman stood on a hill under a full moon. In one hand she held a flask; in the other was an egg which she was pressing to her lips. Under the hill a monstrous black creature was reaching up.

In the second picture the girl was walking with the egg held out in front of her, the creatures was walking along behind her, it wasn't attacking it just seemed to be following.

In the third picture the girl had the egg to her lips and she was pointing to three men armed with swords and shields, each of the men was covered in flames and falling to the ground as the creature attacked them.

'How's she controlling it?' the Major wondered out loud.

'Sound,' Steve and Ethnic answered together.

'It's called the Widows Bell or Widows rattle or Widows flute, it doesn't look like any of those things but it must have had something in common with them for those names to be used.' Red explained.

'Amphibians respond to sound,' Steve elaborated. 'The males call to the females. The Bell can obviously make different types of sound which have different effects on the creature.'

'The Bell has two mouth pieces,' Ethnic carried on. 'Perhaps you blow into it like a flute, one end to summon it and the other to make it attack. In the middle picture she's just holding it out in front of her. Maybe you need to swing it like a Bell or shake it like a rattle, to make the creature follow.'

The Major nodded thoughtfully after a moment. 'You're right I'm sure, sure of it but which mouthpiece summons and which makes it attack?'

Red shook her head, 'There's nothing on that anywhere, I've searched and searched but nothing.' She admitted sadly.

The Major took her hand, 'You've done superbly, wonderfully,' she raised her eyes to include Ethnic and Steve. 'Ten years ago I would have employed the three of you without a second thought.

'Red did most of the work.' Steve and Ethnic mumbled together going a little red.

The Major grinned at them, 'You three are a team, that's obvious to anyone with eyes and a brain.'

'Major you said you'd told the police, what do we do now? - You can't expect us to just leave it, to forget it.' Red asked quietly.

'I had to explain why we were in the house in Usk because the letters changed everything.' The Major began, 'The moment the KGB even ex KGB is mentioned it's no longer a local matter. There are two rival groups of foreign nationals in the area, one with soviet links. A foreign national is found dead, with mysterious chemical burns and an unexplainable wound on his arms and shoulder. From the police and the governments point of view this is not the first time that Russians have assassinated people over here. These assassinations are usually as highly imaginative and as unconventional as they are brutal.'

She looked to the youngsters who all nodded. 'The initial report said that there were chemical burns found on the body and the chemical still hasn't been identified.' She told them. 'The saliva around the bite has been analysed and that also can't be identified but is not dissimilar to several obscure species of Frog. The police and government 'experts' think this has all been concocted in a lab to take advantage of local myths and divert police and press attention. They're warning officers on the ground of an assassin with access to a chemically coated suit and gloves and the conversations between our foreign office and the Russian equivalent have been lively to say the least.'

The Major paused for a moment, obviously searching for the right words. 'You my dears are off the case.' She raised her hand as the three of them started to protest. 'You're clever and you're smart you've unravelled so much of this, it *was* a mystery but now it's dangerous. These people haven't acted on the spur of the moment, this has been planned and organised, they're serious. One man is dead already, this time you have to step back and let the authorities do their job.'

'But . . .' Red started.

'No buts, there's a mystery here which will remain when they've all been caught and deported. If we're right this creature has been around one way or another for centuries. This is something that we can return to when the dust has settled.'

'Hang on! - What about the bell? - they've obviously got it.' Ethnic cut in.

'Technically it's Russian property, so they want it back but it's also evidence. I've been assured that if it's recovered it will be thoroughly examined and analysed whatever happens before it's returned and that's if it's returned. I know the department that will do this, they're thorough and they're good and they owe me a favour. Any sounds that object can make will be recorded and I will have a copy.'

She smiled at the three of them who clearly didn't want to give up. 'We're not beaten yet,' she told them with a warm smile. 'But we do have to wait.'

The Major studied their faces for a moment, then she turned to the boys. 'Imagine how you would feel If anything happened to Jenifer.' She said quietly, then turning to Red, 'Or imagine one of these two getting killed. These men are dangerous, so for now we back off. Promise?'

Red hated admitting defeat but as she glanced at Steve and Ethnic she knew that this time, they had no choice. She nodded solemnly.

Six

Red knew that the Major was right, she'd never really considered the consequences of what they were doing, but the fact that one person had already died was inescapable. It made complete sense to wait until the police had rounded up the two rival groups and after all, she had given the Major her word.

On the other hand there was no point in sitting back and doing nothing. The more information she could find and the more information that she could uncover, the better their chances of success would be when the time was right.

The main problem was that there were two different mysteries that appeared to be linked. The treasure of Monmouth really did exist, she was sure of that. The bipedal amphibian also was to her mind equally real. The two were linked by Argonath and were still linked together now, centuries later. When she looked into the legend of the treasure she discovered information about the amphibian and whenever she tried to learn more about the amphibian she found out more about the treasure.

A few days after they'd left the Major she sent word that the police had rounded up all of the Russian group. The Russians had broken into a disused chapel whilst supposedly working on improvements to the 'Heads of the valleys' road outside Abergavenny. All had an alibi for the date and time of the murder. The police questioned them at length and the decision was made to hold them in custody until they could be deported. No new information had come to light.

On the same day Red discovered that another parcel from Juliet was waiting for her in the Library. This time it was extracts from Baker's commentaries that related to the Argonath volumes that were lost and Juliet wondered if they'd be any help.

Red was sorry to have missed her a second time and emailed her thanks immediately.

The boys appeared as Red had finished working her way through the contents of the parcel.

'Lunch.' Steve shouted from the library entrance as he threw a triangular box labelled Cheese and Tomato across the library to Red.

Red caught it an inch from the monitor screen, 'Bring it don't throw it.' She shouted to Ethnic who was about to launch a bottle of Fanta in the same direction.

'Not more parcels of notes?' Ethnic placed the bottle gently beside Red then opened his own bottle of coke which promptly exploded all over him and Red, getting coke, foam and bubbles all over the papers in front of her.

'Ethnic!' Red shrieked at him, 'What is it with you and bottles?' she frantically wiped the liquid off the paperwork whilst Steve laughed in the corner.

'He was playing catch with the bottle.' Steve laughed.

'I was playing catch with *your bottle,'* Ethnic pointed out then realisation dawned, 'You swapped the bottles?'

'Oh yes.'

'But Mate, we're mates, how could you do that to me?' he protested as he got thumped by Red.

'It's his fault, he swapped the bottle.'

'Ethnic you shook the bottle,' Red thumped him again to make the point. 'It's all over my notes.'

'You mean the notes you're not keeping on the case we're leaving alone.'

'The very same.' Red grabbed Ethnic's cardigan which he'd tied by the sleeves around his waist, she pulled it free and used it as a towel to clean up the mess on the desk.'

'Aw woman come on,' he protested.

'You shook the bottle.'

'It was *his* bottle!'

'Anything there?' Steve asked casually, pointing at the notes when Red had finished. Ethnic knotted the damp and crumpled sleeves of his cardigan around his waist and tried to pat it down.

Red sat back in her chair and carefully fished three pieces of tomato out of her sandwich; she gave two to Steve and threw the third one at Ethnic. 'Yep – I wondered if the gifts constructed by Seren and the gifts left by the Angel were references to the same thing. Even though they're different.'

'Yes I was wondering the same thing myself.' Ethnic lied trying to look informed and interested at the same time as he attempted to worm his way back into Red's good books.

'Both describe a treasure that's practical and intended to help rather than wealth.' Red continued, glaring at Ethnic whilst Steve smirked. 'And Baker came to the same conclusion.

'So an angel or an alien made some stuff as a gift,' Ethnic began.

'And mankind buried it and hid it away for six hundred years.' Steve finished for him. 'But how does the frog fit in to all of this?'

'No idea,' Red answered grabbing her second sandwich, 'It's always there though, the stories about the treasure mention the amphibian and the stories about the amphibian mention the treasure.'

'But it guarded the treasure in some of the stories.' Ethnic chipped in proving he had been paying attention.

'Good point,' Red conceded handing him a piece of tomato this time. 'But how would you get a rare wild predatory creature to behave like a guard dog?'

'One of the gifts let them tame wild creatures didn't it.' Steve remembered as he took the slice of tomato that Red handed him.

'Which would suggest that the gifts and the creature were originally in the same location and probably today are still in the same general area.' Ethnic announced thoughtfully after a moment, finally earning a half smile from Red.

'So we know the general area and we know the creature is an amphibian right?' Steve got the final piece of tomato.

'Which means it's got to be close to water.' Ethnic was on a roll.

'Yeah I thought that but it's not necessarily the case, amphibians aestivate in response to arid conditions, they burrow into the ground. If there's water around it's not going to need to do that.' Red said shaking her head and starting one of her now cheese sandwiches.

'So it could be in a lake or pond?' Steve asked.

'It would have to be a lake or Pond that's been around since medieval times.' Red mumbled through her food.

'What about the rivers?'

'The Usk, Monnow and Wye round here have Trout and Salmon Ethnic,' Steve liked to fish so he already had a good idea of the lakes and ponds in the area. 'The water's going to be shallow and fast over stones. You don't tend to get frogs in those sort of places, they like still-water, ponds and lakes.' he added.

'Okay,' Ethnic wasn't going to admit defeat, 'What about the canal?'

'Too new, only dug two-hundred years ago.' Red told him.

'Are there any old stories or legends connected to lakes or

ponds in the area?' she said through another mouthful of cheese.

'Llangorse lake is supposed to have-'

'Llangorse is too far.'

Steve thought for a moment, 'There's Keepers pond on the top of the Blorenge, they reckon it's got no bottom and Jacko reckons there's a Pike in there the size of-'

'Jacko reckoned Sunderland would qualify for Europe once they got Moyse.'

Red reached for her notebook, 'No I looked up the Keeper's earlier its 19th century, it was dug to provide water for Garnddyrys Forge which was 1817.' She read from her notes, adding, 'that's nowhere near early enough.'

'Okay well there's lots of farm ponds about but most of them have been turned into commercial fisheries, especially around Raglan and Monmouth. They're all small ponds all about ten feet deep max and choc full of Carp.' I've fished most of them; they're all too new and get too many people going to them.' Steve said lowering his voice as a group of third years went past.

'If it's in a Pond or Lake I reckon it'll be somewhere deep and quiet and in the middle of nowhere.'

'I can't think of anywhere round here Red, there's such a small amount of money in farming nowadays that if they've got a pond or lake on their land they'll just fill it with carp and charge people to fish it.'

'Well if it's not in a pond or Lake, it's buried in the ground, how the hell do we find it then?' Red asked as she carefully unscrewed the lid of her pop bottle. To her relief it didn't explode as the drink was ice cold courtesy of the new chilled vending machine recently installed outside the school gym. 'And there's another possibility.'

'Which is?'

'At the time all of this was kicking off, this whole area was pretty lawless.'

'Been into Newport at chucking out time on a Saturday night have you?'

'Yeah, yeah but it was even worse then Ethnic, dozens of ragged little villages, no real protection and organised gangs of outlaws.' Red took a sip of her drink.

'What has this got to do with Kermit?'

'Let me finish Ethnic, and don't start calling it Kermit.' She put the bottle back on the table. 'The outlaws would just help themselves to any food or money that the people had.'

'Sure this wasn't the government?'

'So the people started to hide their stuff away, they dug into the ground and built stone chambers with secret entrances. Then covered them over with soil and they were invisible. 'When the outlaws returned they would take what they could find in the village but they knew nothing of these underground stores.'

'How big were they?' Steve asked thoughtfully.

'Depended on the size of the village, some were quite small others had one or two chambers each the size of a small room.'

'But they were hidden.'

'Yep, if there's any left out there its cos nobody has ever been able to find them.'

'And you think Kermit could be in one of these?'

Red narrowed her eyes fixing Ethnic with her sternest stare, 'The amphibian might be yes, Baker saw the Stalingrad Argonath.'

'Before it was blown up?'

'No Ethnic after it was blown up! Of course before it was blown up,' Red shook her head, 'There's a story in there about one of these underground stores which was called lle cudd or lle claddu and it was haunted, the ghost was described as glistening and with golden eyes.'

'You think that was Kermit?'

Red thumped Ethnic.

'But it doesn't really help does it; it still means that it's hidden underground.' Steve pointed out.

'Yeah I know, these stores were usually near the village rather than in it. But there were loads of isolated villages in the area over the years and some aren't even mentioned on the oldest maps.'

The three of them sat quietly thinking for a moment or two, 'Juliet said that the ordinance survey office used to be in Clarence House in Newport.'

'I think it still is, Remploy's in there I've taken Josh there; it's across the river from the Castle, Multi-storey right next to it. I could get you into it no sweat.' Ethnic told her.

'I might give them a ring and ask if they've got any really old maps of the area.' Red said.

'What about Abergavenny Museum surely they're going to have old maps? Steve wondered out loud.

'Oh but we're missing something here aren't we,' Ethnic said quietly with a smile, he was flying today.

'Go on.' Red and Steve echoed.

'It *was* buried in the ground wasn't it and we already know where, remember what the Major said about the canal breech?'

'Gilwern.' Red and Steve nodded.

'How long's Gilwern been there and is it seven miles from Abergavenny?'

'I'm not sure about the age of the village Ethnic but even if it's a modern village it might have been built on the site of an older one.' Red grinned, 'I can soon found out though.' She said reaching for the keyboard of the Library computer which was still turned off.

'It's not seven miles from Aber mate, more like half that.' Steve pointed out.

'But the measurements can't be accurate and remember Abergavenny itself would have been a heck of a lot smaller back then.' Red argued, 'Ethnic you've excelled yourself hit the switch on the back of the monitor for us.'
'Like I keep telling you,' he said smugly leaning over the monitor to the power switch on the wall behind it. 'Good job I'm here really.' As he turned back one of the trailing arms of his cardigan caught the top of Red's nearly full pop bottle (she hadn't put the top back on) and knocked it forward sending all of its freezing contents down the front of Red's shirt and into her lap.
Her scream could be heard in Chemistry one three blocks away.

By the end of that week all of the remaining Romanians had been rounded up by the police as well. The Major emailed them to say that all of these also had solid alibi's for the night of the murder, but they would also be held for further questioning and then sent to be deported. None of them had the Bell.

Red and the boys were able to get hold of copies of some really old maps of the area but weren't able to pinpoint any likely sites. There was a lot of farmland with many large fields surrounding Gilwern and the fact remained (as Ethnic pointed out) that if Kermit was buried below ground then he could be anywhere.

Over the following weeks the row between the British and Russian foreign offices rumbled on and the Raglan press somehow got hold of the fact that the police had swooped on a number of itinerant workers following a tip off from pupils at Millbrook comp. The scathing headline wasn't likely to do Red or the boys any favours.

A month after their last visit the youngsters returned to Raglan services, as they were later this time, only the sandwich shop was open. A copy of the current Raglan press was hurled onto the table and buried with foot long rolls of chicken tikka and 3 large cups of coke.

Red's own electric wheelchair was in for a service but the school had let her borrow one of the large wheeled self-propelling wheelchairs.

'I reckon we all go and talk to him,' Steve said through a mouthful of roll.

Ethnic shook his head, 'can't talk to the press mate they'll just twist everything you say.'

'Anyone got Deadpool's phone number? - or will he be going after Trump?' Red mumbled through her drink.

'Do you reckon,' Steve started with a smirk, 'If anyone tries to shoot Trump his bodyguards will shout Donald - duck!'

Red choked on her Coke as the three of them burst out laughing.

They made their way through their meals and drink chatting cheerfully, as the eating area slowly emptied around them. Soon only one other person was left, a young strongly built fair-haired man of around 20. He wore tatty jeans, a tee shirt, and a long and heavy black coat. Slowly he rose from his table and walked over to theirs, he had a Raglan Press under his arm.

Ethnic noticed him first, 'Blimey does he want our autograph?' he asked the others.

The man calmly took a chair from the nearest table and dragged it over to theirs. Wordlessly he pulled his wallet out of his back trouser pocket and took out two small square colour photos. He returned the wallet and put his newspaper flat on his lap as he sat down at their table.

He carefully placed the two photos down onto the table. One was a head and shoulder photo of a little boy with curly black hair laughing at the camera. The other was of a young and very pretty woman with long dark hair cradling the same child in her arms.

The man spoke softly and with (as Red and the boys instantly noticed) an east European accent. 'Alin and Ileana, they are my world. Please understand it is not normally in my nature to hurt or to threaten anybody.' He reached into one of the large pockets of his coat, drawing something out and sliding it under his newspaper. 'But for them,' he nodded at the pictures, 'I would do anything.'

He looked at Ethnic, who was the closest to him and then down at the newspaper on his lap. 'Ethnic's eyes followed as the man drew the newspaper back with one hand to reveal that he now had a gun in the other under the table pointing at Red. 'Do not make any noise, you will do exactly what I tell you, I really don't want to hurt any of you but believe me, if I have to I will.' He whispered.

'He's got a gun.' Ethnic hissed.

The three of them looked around helplessly, the Greggs and Starbucks were shut. There were two girls in Subway collecting up the tubs of sandwich filling and an elderly cleaner with a mop on the other side of the room.

'There is no help for you here, my name is Alexis just do what I ask and I'll set you free unharmed.' He picked up the photo of the boy and held it up to them. 'I swear to you on my boy, I swear to you on Alin, I'll not harm you if you do what I ask.'

Red stared at the man in disbelief; her heart was pounding in her ears. Ethnic (on her right) looked like he's going to be sick.

'Put the gun down first,' Steve said trying to sound as calm as he could and not taking his eyes off the gun.

'I'll put the gun in my pocket.' Alexis returned the gun to his pocket but kept his hand in the pocket on the gun.

'What is it that you want us to do?' Red whispered.

'Come with me.'

He pocketed the pictures and slowly rose from his chair. The boys got up and Red turned her chair around. 'Calmly and quietly to the door then into the car park.' He whispered.

They did as he told them and he followed them out. It was dark outside and raining.

'Across to the far side of the car park.'

As they did so their mind's were racing, there was nobody around and apart from the buzz of the traffic on the nearby road, it was silent. They soon reached the other side of the car park where there was an old black battered Ford Transit.

'We're not getting in there.' Red was panicking now.
Alexis pulled the gun from his pocket, 'I have nothing to lose and I will shoot you dead one after the other, if you don't do what I tell you.'
Steve leapt forward between Red and Alexis holding up his hand. '
Mate, calm down - its ok there's no need for this.'
Ethnic stepped up beside Steve, 'C'mon mate, take it easy.'
Keeping the gun on the three of them, he half turned and opened the unlocked back door of the transit.
'Lift her Inside.'
'We're not leaving her.' Steve and Ethnic told him together.
For the first time Alexis smiled, 'I know, I need the three of you.'
He motioned for them to get in. The boys lifted Red's chair aboard then climbed in beside her.
'Your phones please, you'll get them back.'
'I haven't got mine.' Ethnic blurted.
'Nice try but you're western teenagers, you've always got them.' He held out his hand and reluctantly they gave him their phones.
Alexis shut the doors behind him and they heard the clunk of a padlock being closed. A moment later the engine started and the driver's door slammed as the van pulled away.
The back of the van was tatty and completely empty apart from the broken plastic lid of a toolbox, the boys kept Red's chair from tipping and they tried to work out where they're going.
'Please tell me you've still got your old phone in your bag' Ethnic whispered, Red shook her head, she and Ethnic

looked pale and worried sick, Steve was concentrating hard.
'He's turned off the 449 – up to the roundabout by the castle - third exit where's – isn't that?-'
'The road with the garden centre.' Red told him.
Soon the van turned
'Bettws Newydd road?' Ethnic wondered.
'No, no it's the one after it, the road to whatsit?'
'Oh yeah no worries we're trapped in the back of a van by a nutter with a gun and we're on the road to whatsit.
'Guys focus, we can't be far from where the Major lives.'
'You reckon he's after her as well?' Steve actually hoped he would be, not because he wanted her exposed to the danger more because he was sure she'd know what to do.
'Don't know,' Red answered, 'that's another left, that'll take us down to . . . you know that garden centre?'
'We've just gone *past* the garden centre'
'Not that one, the *other* garden centre, the little one opposite the church.
Both boys shook their heads. The van carried on and then they heard a train, very close to them, running parallel to them it seemed, then they turned right and then right again. Soon, about fifteen minutes after they'd got into the van, it slowed down and they felt it reverse and then stop.
Alexis opened the back doors, 'Now come into the house quietly' he whispered.
The boys lowered Red onto the drive where they were now parked. It wasn't at all like what they'd imagined; the drive belonged to a pleasant white wood and brick semi-detached house. One of several nestled around a cul-de-sac, all of the neighbouring houses had their curtains drawn tightly

together and it was still raining. Alexis ushered them through a narrow back door.

'Sorry for the step.' He directed them into the kitchen which seemed oddly warm and welcoming after the back of the transit. Steve and Ethnic expertly bumped Red over the step and they entered the large bright room. A wooden table covered with papers dominated the middle of the room, on top of the papers a large pewter egg with two mouthpieces was being used as a paperweight.

'You know what that is don't you?' he said following Red's eyes.

He was the other side of the table and gestured for the boys to pull up a chair and place them either side of Red. He held up the gun and then carefully and deliberately placed it down on the counter top behind him and took a step away from it. 'I promise I'll only use it if I have to.'

'That's the Bell,' Red couldn't take her eyes off it.

'Cantand cheia in my country, the singing key. The museum called it Ora, Nico called it Dal. Like in your country it had many different names I suppose because nobody really knew what it was.'

'I like Dal . . .' Red gestured towards it, 'Can i?'

Alexis smiled, 'Course you can, here' he picked up the Dal and handed it to her.

The Dal was exactly as Vivian had described it and it looked almost new. The silver gleamed under the kitchen fluorescent as Red carefully turned it in her hands. It truly was a thing of beauty, she'd read so much about it but now to be able to hold it and examine it. The engraving was exquisite at its base a sea of sharp stylised waves rose up into a sky full of stars; it was delicately and beautifully done. The two mouthpieces looked like they were made from reed and had been coated in something that looked like varnish. She was holding history in her hands and it was with great reluctance that she finally placed it back on the tabletop.

'We were told you were all arrested.' Steve broke the silence..

Alexis nodded, 'Those that came over last year yes but some of us were already here.

'Where are the others?' Red asked quietly.

'Dead, all dead, only me now'.

Red was startled, 'Was it the creature, how many have been killed now?'

'Four, Three of us and a pensioner fishing late on the canal. Nobody's noticed that he's missing yet still it's only been a fortnight!' he snorted, then softening his tone he added, 'We tried to help him but his heart stopped, it was the burns. It's always the burns. They're all buried beside the bridge.'

Alexis opened the fridge and pulled out a bottle of lager and held it up to them. 'You want one?'

They shook their heads as he took a bottle opener from a draw and sent the top spinning into the bin.

'The smallest touch and it gets in your system. We tried antiseptic creams, barrier creams, burn creams but nothing worked, nothing touched it.'

Red's interest was starting to overcome her panic, 'You've seen the creature? - Where is it, when did you see it?'

'In my country we call them copii de apă, the water

children, very rare, very secretive. Few know of them, fewer believe. Nico was researching them for the university, he wanted to know if they lived in the legends of any other countries and he found them here in Wales.'

'What? How many, where are they?' Red demanded.

Alexis grinned, 'All in good time. Back in the fourteenth century the Earl of Stafford built a Castle on the banks of the Usk in Newport. During the build his men disturbed a creature hiding deep in the mud, a creature like a huge heavily built black Eel over five feet long.' Alexis paused to take a long swig from the bottle.

'An Eel? - The descriptions we've uncovered are completely different to that.

'Yeah bipedal,' Ethnic added hoping he at least sounded like he knew what he was talking about.

Alexis nodded, 'Our group, the first of us, included a biologist, Ben. He and Nico had worked out that all of the different accounts described the creatures in one of two ways. Nico found a drawing that had been owned by Rasputin of an eel like creature half way between a Lungfish and an Axolotil. This creature had also been found buried in mud, this one near the mouth of the Danube. It was very sluggish and the locals killed it but all of the people that had handled it became very sick afterwards and within a week most of them had died. There were other accounts as well, dotted through history of great black eel like creatures that buried themselves in river mud. You sure I can't get you something?'

'You got any coke,' Steve had come to the conclusion that the guy probably really didn't want to hurt them and his

mouth was very dry.
'Alexis opened the fridge, got lemonade, ginger ale and 7up.'
'Um 7up I think please.'
'Can I have some ginger ale,' Ethnic chipped in.
Red stared at them in disbelief, then Alexis turned to her, 'Um yeah, lemonade please.' She managed after a moment; the evening was becoming more surreal by the moment.
'Nico thought that the eel-like creatures were the larval stage, the tadpoles if you will but Ben realised that these were the males.' Alexis carefully handed out the drinks he'd just poured. 'In the Argonath they described the creature as looking like a woman and actually they were right, for the wrong reason but right. This creature, the biped is the female. The legs, the upper thighs, like all amphibians are heavy and muscular but the waist is thin, if you get a glimpse of the standing creature the impression is female rather than male but in truth the males and females are completely different.
'Do both males and females feed on blood?' Steve was enjoying his drink now and felt a lot calmer (although his eyes kept wandering to the gun)
Alexis smiled, 'No, no they eat fish, Bream seems to be favourite. The blood thing is more about defence or when they wake from aestivation.' He took another swig from the bottle. 'These things were around with the dinosaurs, lot's of big predators most of them bipedal lizards. Thick scaly skin, the amphibians in comparison are delicate, their skin is moist and permeable, they need an angle, a mechanism, something to give them an edge. They feed on fish, which

they catch and swallow but to survive they're going to need to fight and to be able to hold their own against monsters.'
'Poison skin like arrow frogs. Their skin kept them safe?' Ethnic said.
Alexis pointed his bottle at Ethnic, 'That's part of it; you're right but remember their enemies are lizards, thick scaly skin, not as easily burnt as ours. Poisonous skin is a defence but it's secondary, their primary defence is to attack and their attack is like nothing you've ever seen. Believe me if you ever see it, you'll never forget it.' he went visibly paler and took another long swig emptying the bottle.
There was a noise, the creak of a floorboard above them.
'Is there somebody else here?' Red asked looking upwards.
Alexis shrugged his shoulders, 'No just me now and the cat upstairs.'
'You don't sound like a terrorist.' Steve said quietly.
Alexis burst out laughing, 'Terrorist? - I'm a teacher! An English teacher or at least I was going to be.' He pulled up a seat and sat opposite them on the other side of the table. Further away, Steve and Ethnic noticed, from the gun on the counter behind him and to his right.
'I was training over here; my family have always spoken English so it was a logical thing for me to do. I knew Nico and Ben well; Nick had been planning this for years. I managed to get placed in Newport on a work exchange project, Nico and Ben started putting together a team, I rented this.' He pointed around him. 'Nick the place in Usk, we knew the treasure was here and it was, we knew that we'd find it and we did.'
The fact their kidnapper was a teacher brought the three of

them considerable relief, even with a gun he was not now as intimidating as he had been a few moments previously. True he'd kidnapped them at gunpoint but a teacher was still *just* a teacher. There was always a way to handle a teacher.

'You found the treasure?' Red was all questions now.

'And what about the KGB?' Ethnic added.

'You three don't disappoint, 'Yes we found the treasure.' He nodded to Red, 'and they're ex KGB there's a difference. Okay,' he moved forward in his chair. 'Three of us come over first, we get to know the area, where are the jobs, who's looking to hire. We want outside jobs in the area, outside jobs because we know how to find the treasure just not where. It's seven miles from Abergavenny but we don't know in which direction. We do know though certain features around the site, things to look for on the surface. There's a Russian Andrei who knows about the treasure, he starts off helping but he gets greedy. He and Nic fall out, so he sets up his own team but Nico's seen this coming and makes sure he gets the Dal first. Without the Dal you can't claim the treasure.'

'You know how the Dal works and why it works?' Red asked him.

'Yes we know why it works (his eyes fell on the device) that's not the difficult bit. Anyway we're all over here and we'd narrowed the location down to three sites, all in Monmouthshire all pretty much in the middle of nowhere.'

'So you just started to dig?' Steve asked.

'Didn't even need to do that mate.' He rose from his chair and walked over to the back door, beside which was an umbrella holder holding two umbrellas and half a dozen thin metal poles. He drew out one of the rods and returned to the table. 'Greatest undiscovered treasure in history and that's all you need to find it.' he handed the rod to Steve. 'Well that and Google maps!'

The pole was aluminium about five feet long and thin; it had the diameter of a pencil. The one end had been sharpened and it was stained with earth.

'The treasure is hidden in a long chamber, stone walls, ceiling and floor, like an underground tunnel. There's up to four feet of soil above it, from the ground it's invisible but archeologists have discovered that if there's something hidden underground then there's usually signs above ground if you know what you're looking for.'

Steve agreed, 'Yeah they found a Roman Villa near Caerleon from patterns in crops spotted from a plane.'

'Yep anything looked promising on the maps we'd visit the site with a drone and get higher res pictures from the air. If it still looked a likely site we'd probe with those, 'he pointed at the pole Steve was holding. 'If it went all the way in, you'd move forward a yard and try again. If you hit something solid then you'd investigate.'

'How does the creature fit into all of this?' It was Red's turn to interrupt.

'The treasure is in the chamber and the chamber is where the creature lives.' Red and the boys looked at each other open mouthed. 'This is how it worked; Nico had most of the information from libraries at home. He was sure the treasure was in Monmouthshire then he finds out about the Argonath bequest. The remaining books he needs have been given to a school in Monmouthshire, Millbrook. It was like a sign. I went to the school on a day off and found they were looking for gardeners. The opportunity was too good to miss, he brings the plan forward, he comes over and gets the job at your school. He soon knows the layout, knows the security, knows the warden knows his rounds, and knows where all the keys are and he can get into the library when the school is shut.'

'I knew someone had been looking at those books.' Red gasped.

'Yes he mentioned you often; he couldn't believe that nobody else was interested in them. Anyway he puts the information from Millbrook with what he already knows, every scrap of information there is on the creatures. Then Ben fills in the gaps and we realise, that this creature, our creature, is bound to the treasure.'

'How?'

'Ben worked it out; the creatures are rare, rarer than rare. Some here in Wales, some in Hungary and that's it. One male and two or three females in each case, all that's left of them in the world. The male buries himself in thick tidal mud. Most amphibians keep to freshwater, these it seems are able to tolerate at least some salt in the water. These males have an incredibly slow metabolism; they do next to nothing, just feeding up when they need to.'

'That's so typical,' Red's quip drew angry glances from Ethnic and Steve. 'Sorry, please carry on, the males do nothing all day and?'

Alexis grinned. 'They pretty much stay in the same place, they keep to the mud and if they come up at all it's only at night and only when it's quiet. The females move upriver and separate, each will have her own territory. The females will never stray too far from a water source, usually burrowing into the bank deep below the surface. They go out of their way to avoid man, man is bipedal so to them that means predator but if they're discovered they'll fight and when that happens there's only ever one outcome.'

'Go on.'

'The attack is in two stages the first stage is - is difficult to explain, the first stage is to subdue. Once this is done they take the blood. There are four hooked teeth in the centre of the roof of the mouth. These teeth are hollow, like fangs it pushes them through the skin and drinks the blood.'

Red wasn't impressed, 'Oh god that's horrible.'

'You think so? - That's not the worst of it. When we discovered the chamber we knew we'd discovered the treasure but we'd discovered the creature as well. Tomo and James wanted to kill it. Nico and Ben said no, we'd use the Dal. When we entered the chamber there was a nest, you know how tree frogs build a nest of foam for their eggs?'

Red and the boys nodded.

'It was like that but the size of an armchair, a sort of web of thick oily bubbles and foam all bunched up in the corner. The creature was inside it curled up into a ball. You can stand in that part of the chamber and we were stood right by it, lights and torches, it didn't bat an eyelid. We crept out quietly to decide what to do but Tomo went back, he wouldn't listen, he took that. (Alexis' eyes flicked to the gun.)'We were right behind him, chasing after him but it's cramped down there, you're on your knees, he meant her harm and she knew it and she can move so fast. She leapt into him, then she's on his back wrapping her legs round his waist. He's still on his knees; she grabs his arms and presses her mouth into the back of his neck. Her mouth is soft it takes the shape of whatever it's pressed into. 'There was pain in his eyes now from the memory and the emotion that it generated was clearly still raw. 'It looked like a kiss, he's on his knees, she on his back wrapped round him. Everywhere that her skin touches his, his skin is burning, melting under her touch and he's just kneeling there and saying the same thing over and over'

'What?' Red whispered.

Alexis looked her in the eyes, 'He said I can see, she's showing me and I can see, don't stop her, don't hurt her, I can see. None of us could move, none of us could do anything. He was dead in three minutes.'

Ethnic had had enough. 'Okay time out, you're not going to shoot us, we're out of here. He got up and made for the back door.

Alexis had the gun against Red's temple in barely two seconds. 'You're forgetting my family, our families, Nico's, James', Tomo's. I'm all that's left now, if I fail, all that work, all that loss is for nothing.' He snapped.

Steve grabbed Ethnic and threw him back into the chair. 'Take the gun off her now.' Steve was furious but helpless whist Alexis had the gun.

Alexis kept hold of the gun but pointed it away from Red. 'You have no idea, cell phones, social media, fast-food.' He snapped back matching Steve's anger. 'You know Nico was one of the *top* researchers in our country, an academic but he could earn well over *twice* as much working over here as a gardener. You have so much, you waste so much. Our families have to survive on next to nothing. Where I live there is little work, no prospects. The treasure was for the people, to teach them, empower them. It gives control, real control but you hid it away, buried it in the ground. Gifts are made to be used. I'm sorry but your country has forgotten this. It's been lying in the ground for six hundred years, if you won't use it, if you won't claim it. Then we will.'

'How did the others die?' Steve said, more calmly this time.

Alexis lowered the gun and slowly and deliberately put it back on the worktop. 'James was beside Tomo when he died, they were like brothers. None of us could move, she gets in your head, nothing works properly you can't think straight. People used to think they used magic, that they were creatures of magic but Ben worked that out as well. It was a pheromone, a narcotic; whenever they fought they won because whatever they fought never wanted to fight back.'

'Ben explained it to James, he told him and he told him. We thought he'd got it, thought he understood but it played on his mind, got into his head. When she took Tomo he dropped the gun, it was on the floor right in front of James. James couldn't pick it up so afterwards he was racked with guilt and he couldn't get what Tomo said out of his mind. Later that night, he crept out and went back to her. We found him the following morning.

The proximity of the gun to her head had reminded Red in no uncertain terms of the predicament that they were in. Despite that, she was desperate to find out all that she could. 'What did you do?' she asked whilst telling herself over and over that he was just a teacher.

'Ben went back with Nico that night just to watch her; she didn't attack them because she knew they were no threat. So they explored the chamber, our entrance is at the one end, the creature is pretty much in the middle and the other end is where the treasure is but it had collapsed. Two centuries ago they dug the canal through the county, they'd come within feet of the treasure. They didn't find it but their excavations collapsed the far end of the chamber. So for the next few nights we started to clear the earth, the creature ignored us as long as we left her alone. It was difficult work because the space was so cramped and we had to take the cleared soil and dump it where it wouldn't be noticed.'

'And the others that died?'

'Vasile tripped and fell, his hand struck the creature, she didn't respond she knew he wasn't attacking her. But her poison got on his skin, that's all it takes just a touch. Ben and Nico tried to clean the wound, they tried everything but it's over in minutes.'

'And the Pensioner?'

Was in the wrong place at the wrong time. When we first started working in the chamber she just stayed in her nest but as time went on she started becoming more active. Near the entrance to the chamber there's a small opening, a hole leading up to the surface. It's not large but she can squeeze through. Ben followed her one night and watched her feed. She sat on the edge of the canal with just her fingertips in the water. He said the fish just came to her, she'd grab one, swallow it, then another would come, like they were queuing up to be eaten. On the evening we finally cleared the debris from the collapsed tunnel, we heard a scream from outside, me and Ben went out and we found him. He'd been fishing and was carrying his gear back to his car. He literally fell over her in the dark. We tried to help him but there was nothing that we could do. He kept thanking us, telling us he'd be okay if we could just get him home but when we got him to his feet his heart stopped.'

Red frowned, 'You said the creature went out of his way to avoid people, why did she let him get that close?'

'Yes, Ben couldn't understand that either. He thought that it was probably our fault. We'd been in the chamber pretty much every night for a fortnight. The creature had become accustomed to us, we weren't a threat and we'd pretty much left her alone. Ben figured that normally she'd aestivate until there was flooding, the metabolism was so slow and the animal so large, in comparison to other amphibians, that he reckoned it would be for decades if not longer. We'd woken her, disturbed her but then we both sort of got used to each other, we were just a harmless biped which she now knew that she could deal with if necessary.'

'You said that this creature was bound to the treasure, do you mean that they're both in the same place?' Yet again insatiable curiosity overcame Red's panic. She'd spent weeks thinking and puzzling over the creatures and the treasure and the answers were here, now.

'No, I meant the creature is bound to the treasure.'

'Bound to the treasure?'

'This creature is not the Widows creature; not the Tretower creature but it *is* family, maybe a sister, more likely a daughter or granddaughter. Seren understood these creatures; he must have done to make the Dal. To make the

Dal he must have encountered a male as well as a female. Ben reasoned that they lived separate lives only coming together to breed. The male would swim upriver calling to his females as he went. A female on hearing him would respond, would call back then follow his call to him. They would mate underwater and then she would carry her eggs back to her den. Her nest in the chamber is foam, like a tree frog, many species of these carry the eggs to a safe place. The tadpoles consume the egg cases and are then returned to the water by the female. Seren had followed the female and knew where her den was, he'd heard the sound that both frogs made and made the Dal to mimic these. Ben figured that two of the sounds were based on the male, the sounds that call and get her to follow. The third sound, the one that makes her attack, is the females response call, this would make her think that another female was in her territory, which would provoke her to attack.'

Red stared at him open mouthed. 'But we don't know which is which?'

Alexis grinned, 'We did, let me continue, You've diligently studied the Argonath volumes, those at your school even the one that had been loaned to Abergavenny but you missed one, our fault I'm afraid, sorry about that.'

'What, how?'

'Caldicot has a super modern library, popular with the community loads of different groups, lots of events going on and currently home to the Argonath volume six on loan from Millbrook. Of interest to them due to its tales of Gregory.'

Red was cross now, 'It would have been on the list on the

board in the Library. All the books loaned out are on . . .'
'On a printed A4 sheet on the notice board over the computer and printer in the corner. The same printer that printed the sheet in the first place.
'You altered the sheet!' Red was outraged.
'You talked a lot to Nico didn't you?'
Red blushed as both boys look at her questioningly; she'd failed to mention this.
'Nico saw your interest and saw how you three could solve puzzles. You may not believe me but he wanted to keep you safe. We want the treasure for our families the Russians want the power that the treasure will give them. We could look after ourselves.' He nodded toward the gun. 'You three, with respect, would have got hurt.'
'So what do you want us for?' Red finally asked the one question she'd been avoiding.
'I'll come to it. Nico liked your interest and he hated misleading you but he'd intended putting it right but events over took him.'
Alexis deliberately caught Steve's eye and after a moment Steve nodded as he understood.
'Seren's made the Dal, he waits a few weeks and he takes Marianna –'
'Marianna?'
'The maiden later the widow, the girl he married. He takes her back to the creature's lair. She sits outside and calls the creature to her then leads it away from the nest. Seren enters the lair and finds 3 egg cases. Each one looks like two huge leaves, one above the other joined at the edges. He opens one carefully, inside there's foam and a partially formed egg in

the middle. He takes it outside, throws the egg and foam into the river but he keeps the egg case. He signals to his wife who leads the creature back. He tells Marianne that if there's ever trouble in the future and he's not around she's to put the treasure in the case and hide it in the lair. He also tells her how to use the creature to kill her enemies.'

Alexis turned to Red and the boys waiting for a question but this time none are forthcoming.

'There's a second account about Marianna's bell. This time it's a granddaughter and she used the Dal to confront a gang of mercenaries attacking her village. This is what's depicted in the Brecon window. She led the creature from its lair to an Inn that had been requisitioned by the Mercenaries. When there were none left alive she led it back. Years later when she was a grandmother herself she and her daughter called upon the creature again when a local Nobleman's son started persecuting the villagers with his thugs. Again none were left alive.'

'What happened with Nico?'

'I wondered when you'd ask. So the tunnel had collapsed, we spent a couple of weeks getting all the debris and shoring up the walls around it. We removed the stones from the floor and there's the egg case with the treasure inside it. We started to clear the soil around it but then she starts getting agitated, she's out of her nest just squatting there watching us. Ben said if we tried to move it she'd attack, he reckoned the females stayed with the eggs until they hatched to defend them. We weren't a threat to her, she knew this but if we threatened her eggs she was going to attack.'

Alexis pulled up the chair again and slowly sat down. 'We tried the Dal but it didn't work so Ben rubbed a stick across her back to collect some of the poison. He and Nico went back to your school in the nights to try and produce a barrier or antidote in the chemistry lab.'

'Ben's read up on poison frogs. With what he knew, and the sample he had, he finally produced something that might have worked but there was no way to test it.'

'Nico's always been in charge, so he took the responsibility. We'd always had another solution but we wanted to do the right thing first.

He told us that we were to go into town for the night, a last night out. Then the following day we'd end it one way or another. We met up in town in the Chicks; Nico sent a message saying he was going to be late so we waited.'

Red narrowed her eyes, 'But he didn't show?'

'No we realised eventually that he'd gone in alone. We raced back but there was no sign of him but the treasure was still there and his car had gone. We found his body back at the school behind the sports shed he must have been trying to get to the chemistry lab.'

'The chemistry labs are nowhere near the sports shed.' Ethnic pointed out.

'No we figured he was disorientated, he'd been bitten and burnt. God knows how he'd gotten away from her or been able to drive. It was getting light so we had to hide him. We'd always intended to hide the treasure at the school once we'd found it.'

'The pit?'

'Yep we hid his body there meaning to go back the night after but they found his body in the morning and everything went pear-shaped.
So me and the others kept our heads down. We stayed away from the chamber, then suddenly the police are rounding up everyone. They get Ben, he tells them he's staying in Usk but knows nothing, they've got the time of death wrong. The police reckon Nico was killed in the evening when we were all in town but he was still warm when we found him at 5am. There's no link to me and they've got everyone else. I'm all that's left now but we'd already decided what to do. None of us could work the Dal but there might be a reason. Otherwise I've got another solution to the problem.'
He went over to a cabinet and carefully pulled a drawer open taking out and holding up a dark green egg shaped object. A hand-grenade.
'This was our final solution, now we try the Dal one last time, if it doesn't work this time then this ends tonight.' He placed the grenade next to the Dal; they are both the same size and shape.
'The Dal didn't work?' Red asked.
'The sixth Argonath volume tells you how to use it. Except we can't make it work, look.' Alexis leant forward picking up the Dal, he took a deep breath and blew hard first through one mouth piece and then the other. Finally he held it out at arm's length and shook it.
Each time it made a different sound, a sort of dry rattle, a different pitch through each mouth piece and when shaken but still a rattle more than anything else.
'After what happened to Tomo we took this in there, tried

all three ways no reaction nothing. That's to call, to summon, (he pointed to the top mouth piece) you shake it to get the creature to follow and blow into the other one to make it attack.

'But what do you expect us to do? - You know more than we do.' Steve asked finally, silently fearing the answer.

'Ben rang me the morning before he was arrested. He told me we'd all been stupid and he knew what to do and to meet him at the tunnel with the Dal. But he never turned up, the police had got him.'

'Why didn't he just tell you over the phone?' Steve asked exasperated.

'Because you never know who might be listening, where I'm from you learn to be cautious especially when it comes to what we're seeking and who's looking to steal it.' Alexis waved his arms like this was obvious. 'Ben said we'd all been stupid, like anyone of us should have been able to work it out. Then I got to thinking that in all the cases in history it was a woman who'd used the Dal, one even taking a daughter with her when she had two sons.'

'Oh wait a minute, if you mean Red, over my dead body - .' Steve turned to Red, but Red was miles away.

Red had worked it out, the second she'd heard the Dal she'd known instantly that it was both right and wrong at the same time. She remembered a biology lesson from the previous year. In the class lab, along with some mice and stick insects were George and Mildred. George and Mildred lived in a large plain tank with a small heater and some pondweed. The teacher had asked Jade to top up the tank but she hadn't done it the way that she was supposed to. The effect (on George at least) was instant and as she remembered she understood.

Alexis was staring at Red as the realisation dawned upon her.

'You know don't you I can see it all over your face.'

Red knew that there's no point in trying to lie. 'Oh you idiots, yes I'm sorry but you have been a little bit stupid.' Despite the situation that she was in she couldn't stop herself from grinning, 'I know how to make the Dal work.'

<u>Seven</u>

Less than an hour later the four of them left the van on an old stone bridge and headed down onto the canal towpath. There was a small turning circle in the canal near the canal bridge. On the far bank was a line of tightly planted trees, on the near bank there were a few trees with open fields behind. The moon was full and bright but it was still raining.

The towpath had recently been resurfaced so Red was able *just* to manage with her wheelchair.

Alexis and Ethnic led with Steve and Red following along the narrow path behind them.

'This is not a good idea, there's too much that can go wrong and we're stuck in the middle of nowhere.' Steve whispered to Red.

'We don't have a choice; he'll just blow it up otherwise.' Red said firmly.

'But what if . . .'

'Mate, he's right the Dal will either work or it won't. If it does we've got control if it doesn't we're out of here.'

Steve thought for a moment, 'We could use the Dal to . . .'

'Set the creature on him? – Could you do that?'

Steve couldn't answer.

'Me neither.' Red whispered.

'Here, we stop here.' Alexis stopped, pulled a torch from his pocket, and pointed to a knot of small trees. 'There.' He scrambled over a low rusty wire fence that was a tangle of ivy and brambles and gestured for Ethnic to follow.

The plants also covered the floor on the other side. Alexis

shone his torch at the ground and after a moment grabbed something and pulled.

He lifted a square wooden frame, covered in ivy and brambles from the ground. 'You like? Three by three wooden frame with pond liner stretched across it like a canvas. Brambles and ivy fixed to the top and it's invisible when it's on the ground.'

He leant the cover against a tree and pointed to the ground where the cover had been. A large circular hole was now visible. 'We go in here; if the Dal works she'll come out there.' He pointed the beam to another (much smaller) hole, like a rabbit hole. It was barely visible, even with the torch. 'Right now we try, if it works and she comes, hold the Dal like this and gently shake it.' He demonstrated holding his arm out straight and delicately shaking the Dal. 'Shake it gently and she'll move slowly. If she comes lead her in that direction,' he pointed back towards a (just visible in the moonlight) second bridge a hundred yards or so beyond the one that they'd just left.

'The path is straight when you reach that bridge stop and don't make a sound and whatever you do don't wish her harm.'

Ethnic looked at the smaller hole, 'This is tiny, how'd she get out of here?'

'Let's see shall we, 'he handed the Dal to Red, 'It's the short upper Mouthpiece to summon.'

Red carefully took the Dal.

Alexis turned back to Ethnic, 'You're with me – down you go.' He pointed to the large hole.

Ethnic was clearly not thrilled by the prospect of clambering

down into the dark hole; he looked helplessly over to Red and Steve on the other side of the fence.
Alexis handed him the torch, 'Y'see that root along the edge? Grab that stick your legs in and drop keeping hold of the root then when you let go you're only a couple of feet above the floor.'
Ethnic stuck the torch in his mouth and sat on the edge of the hole then he grabbed the root and slid in. For a moment he hung from the root before dropping through to the ground. Alexis followed him in.

Red and Steve watched them go and then found themselves alone on the canal bank.
Steve turned to Red, 'okay – now what?'
Red handed him the Dal, 'quickly go and hold it underwater.'
Steve took it to the canal and carefully dunked it into the water, a mass of bubbles streamed to the surface then nothing.
'Okay – now what?' he asked.
'Lift it out, hold it up.'
Steve did so and was surprised to see that the water inside it didn't run out despite the mouthpiece on the bottom of the egg.
'Remember George and Mildred?'
'The Frogs in Biology yes,' Steve remembered.
George and Mildred were a pair of Xenopus aquatic frogs often seen in colleges and labs.
'Mr Dobbs asked Jade to top up their tank once, she was supposed to pour the water in slowly but you know Jade.

Anyway she just tips it in and George went mental. He's swimming round the tank making this noise.'

'Ok . . . ?'

'Y'see they're programmed to breed when there's a flood, the males call to the females. When Alexis blew into the Dal the noise it made was like the noise that George made but it was different because . . .'

Steve grinned, 'Because George was underwater.'

'What did their biologist say, the males come up the river calling to the females, they'll be underwater. Then there's the picture, remember she had the Dal in one hand and a flask in the other.'

'She had water in the flask, oh God this is going to work isn't it?'

'Let's find out shall we.'

Red raised the short mouthpiece to her lips.

Ethnic paused a moment getting his bearings. Alexis dropped in beside him and reached for something in the wall to the side. A moment later to Ethnic's amazement a string of white Christmas tree lights flickered into life lighting up the tunnel.

They were powered by a car battery and strung out along the length of the tunnel. The tunnel was long narrow and low. Only in the middle section was it possible to stand, the tunnel was an 'L' shape with the right angle bend in the middle. The section that Ethnic and Alexis were in was high enough for them to kneel only.

Ethnic looked around him and whistled in appreciation, 'This is incredible.' The walls, floor and ceiling were all made from long rough stones jammed up against each other. The rain still falling through the hole sparkled and glistened in the Christmas lights, it was magical. 'You've got lights down here that's amazing.'

'No that's the amazing bit.' Alexis pointed to the middle of the high section where a huge mass of oily foam and bubbles covered the floor and the walls in the corner.

Ethnic suddenly remembered why they were there, 'Is she in there?'

'Yes don't be afraid, don't wish her harm.'

Ethnic had no intention of wishing her harm at all; he was torn between fear and wonder. 'What happens now?'

'We wait, if your friends can work the Dal, she'll leave through there.' He pointed to a gap between the wall and ceiling with the torch. 'If not the three of you are free to go, I'll drive you to a hotel a mile from here you'll get help there. I'll come back and finish the job.' Alexis said grimly.

'Won't the grenade destroy the treasure?'

'This part of the tunnel is straight. The treasure is round the corner in the other arm of the tunnel. In the First World War they found that right angled bends in trenches helped to contain explosions to one section. The treasure is round the corner and i've covered it in rubble to protect it. Because my intention when I moved it was to protect it, she knew I meant it no harm so she left me alone.'

'But if you come back with the grenade won't she know?'

'That's why I'm using the grenade and not the gun. I'm not coming in here I can chuck it into the hole from the bank, it's a really short fuse, it'll be over before she knows what's going on.'

'If it comes to that will you let me see her first and take a picture for Red?'
'Your phones are in the glove-box of the van, I'll bring you and Steve back down here so you can both take pictures for Jenifer.'
Suddenly the silence around them was broken, the noise was clearly the same as the Dal made before but it had changed. It had a resonance and quality that it didn't have before. As if somebody had run the sound through a tuning device.
Ahead of them the nest of bubbles and foam started to move like a blanket being pushed aside as someone underneath it climbed out of bed.
Alexis was overjoyed, 'Look she's coming! – they've done it, it's working - your friends have done it!.

Back on the bank as Red blew into the mouthpiece she instantly becomes aware of two things, firstly the sound was now completely different, secondly a fine spray of water leaked out of the bottom mouthpiece as she blew into the top one.
She paused for a moment, 'Steve, is there a drink bottle in my bag?'
Seeing the problem Steve quickly opened the backpack on the back of the chair and handed a half full bottle to Red.
'I'm not going to fill it with coke am I?'
'Oh Yeah right – hang on.' He tipped out the contents as he ran back to the canal.
Red kept blowing into the mouthpiece.
Steve returned with the bottle which was full of canal water.

Red paused for a moment, 'Is anything happening?'
Steve went as close as he dared to the rabbit hole, 'Nothing it's just . . . wait a minute, I think something's coming.'

Back in the tunnel Ethnic was kneeling next to Alexis and he couldn't believe what he was seeing.
He'd visualised the creature as a giant Frog but there was so much more to her than that.
Alexis laughed at Ethnic's amazement, 'See do you see? . . . this is why we couldn't, we had to try everything first, look at her, look!'
Ethnic was looking alright, his face was a picture of astonishment.
The creature climbed from her nest and stood a few feet from Ethnic and Alexis, she bobbed her head back and forth slowly, looking to pinpoint the sound.
Ethnic just stared; doubting he could move even if he wanted to, nothing could have prepared him for the site that was before him.

She stood straight but not at all like a human would. She was around four and a half feet tall, her arms and legs looked almost human but her feet were webbed, like a frog's and her fingers ended in discs. From her waist up she looked thin, her ribs visible under her skin, her neck was short and really did appear to have a pulse, as if her heart was indeed in her throat but it was her face and head that demanded Ethnic's attention.
Her huge eyes burned with a fierce intelligence. In the twinkling lights Ethnic saw in her eyes a breathtaking

golden kaleidoscope of colour and shade that seemed to make their surface swim. Opaque eyelids like wet white lace glided over the eyes bottom to top as the creature blinked. There was no obvious nose but two small black holes in the middle he assumed were nostrils. The mouth had no lips and just looked like a line cut into the bottom of the face but extending well around the sides of the head.

The creature's colour was pale at the front getting darker as it extended around to the back. The colours were a grassy green and blue grey swirled together into a circling mottled pattern. The skin was wet and glossy almost as if the creature had been coated in varnish. The whole effect was breathtaking but it was her eyes that overwhelmed the viewer.

Ethnic stared into her beautiful eyes and felt all his anxiety and alarm just drift away. He knew that he was strong, that he had nothing to worry about, nothing to fear. He was here with her and everything else was going to be okay. It would all sort itself out; all that mattered was that he was here with her.

Alexis shook Ethnic, 'Don't look into her eyes for too long, just for a moment.'

The creature looked at Alexis and Ethnic then leapt into the gap in the wall, disappearing in a second.

'Right c'mon move.' Alexis started crawling forward but Ethnic just knelt staring at the spot where she'd been standing.'

Alexis shook him again but more vigorously this time. 'Come on, snap yourself out of it we need to do this quickly, for your friends.'

Ethnic shook his head and followed Alexis. In the middle of the tunnel Alexis stood and started carefully to make his way past the nest and around the corner. 'Don't tread on any of these patches whatever you do.' He said pointing to the floor.

On the floor where the creature had stood were several patches of slime (like wet foot prints).

'They'll be toxic for a couple of hours yet.'

He reached the corner, dropped to his knees and started to crawl into the next section of tunnel. The lights were here also but whereas the previous section had been dry this section was clearly damp. Water dripped from the ceiling onto the rubble and debris that covered the stone floor.

In several places the tunnel has been shored up with timber, bricks and breezeblocks and against the low broken far wall of the tunnel was a dark mass covered with stones and rubble. The treasure of Monmouth.

As Steve stared he suddenly saw movement, he blinked thinking his eyes were deceiving him but no, a hand had appeared, a hand like a child's hand but with the ends of the fingers flattened into discs. The hand was on the grass outside the front of the hole one second and then like a magic trick, the creature appeared almost instantly pulling herself up and out of the ground.

Steve stared at it dumbfounded; Red lowered the mouthpiece from her lips as she too stared at the creature standing before them glistening in the moonlight.

Without thinking she held the Dal out in front of her, arm outstretched and gently shook it, instantly the creature started to move towards her. 'Steve get behind the chair!' she hissed urgently.

Steve didn't move he just stared at the creature which was getting closer to him.

'Steve now!' Red shrieked much louder than she'd intended.

Steve snapped out of it and raced to Red, grabbing the back of the chair.

'I need both hands you'll have to take the chair.' Red gasped.

Steve grabbed the handles and set off under the bridge.

'Slowly, gently,' Red hissed.

Red had hoped that the Dal would stop leaking once she stopped blowing into the mouthpiece but this wasn't the case at all. As the Dal leaked it got lighter and the tone began to change, Red had to top it up by carefully pouring water from the bottle into the mouthpiece on the top of the Dal. Not easy when both of her arms were stretched out in front of her and she's being dragged backwards along the towpath.

Both Red and Steve were in effect moving backwards along the towpath, facing the creature which was moving towards them as they moved away from it. Red struggled to top up the Dal whilst Steve struggled with keeping his eyes on Red and the creature whilst constantly having to crane his neck to look around behind him and make sure he stayed on the path as he pulled the wheelchair along in the darkness.

They proceeded slowly and carefully, the moon was full and bright but a brisk wind caused frequent clouds to drift across it throwing the landscape into almost complete darkness for a few seconds before the moon lit everything up again.

Red and Steve struggled to take their eyes off the creature which appeared to be in a trance, she took a few steps, stopped, paused moving only her head up and down or side to side then a few steps more. Progress was slow but it was progress. Aside from the strange clicking of the Dal, all was silent until something strange happened.

All at once from out of nowhere, somewhere behind them was another sound, the same strange click but slower and deeper.

'Steve what the hell is that?' Red gasped.

'I don't know.' Steve twisted his head around straining his eyes in the darkness, 'It's coming from the bridge we're heading to.'

The creature started reacting to the second sound, her movement became more erratic, the head shaking more violent. She started to speed up and was soon only feet away from Red. Then Red's chair abruptly started to slow down.

Red turned round to Steve. 'Steve move! – What are you doing you can't –'

But Steve had gone.

Back in the tunnel Ethnic and Alexis had removed the rubble and stones and pulled the treasure from its hiding place. It was the size and weight of a large heavy rucksack.

Wordlessly they dragged it back into the middle of the tunnel.

Finally they reached the hole that they had entered through, 'Right you with me, the vans on the bridge we'll get it in there then get your friends.'

Alexis pulled the light cable from the battery and plunged their world into darkness. Above them the moonlight shone and the falling rain shimmered through the hole.

'There's a grab hold half way up but you won't be able to reach, stand up.'

Ethnic was able to stand in the hole.

Alexis cupped his hands, 'Here give me your foot and I'll give you a bunk up.'

'Nothing wrong with your English,' Ethnic put his foot into Alexis's hands and as Alexis pushed him up he was able to scramble up and out of the hole.

'Here take the treasure.' Alexis passed it up so Ethnic could drag it out of the hole, then he climbed out.

'I can hardly hear them.' Ethnic was looking in the direction that Red and Steve went but it was too dark to see anything.

Alexis pulled the cover back over the hole. 'They'll be ok, they've got control, quicker we do this, quicker we get to them, with me.' Alexis hauled the treasure onto his back and they ran to the bridge, their feet slipping and sliding on the wet grass.

They reached the van and opened the backdoors of the transit, the tiny circular light fitted inside the roof filled the interior with feeble, watery white light.

'In that corner' Alexis pointed to the far left hand corner at the back of the cab. Ethnic dragged the treasure into the corner whilst Alexis pulled some straps and clamps from a compartment in the door.

Ethnic now had his first opportunity to have a good look at

what had caused them all so much trouble. The egg cases were indeed shaped like two giant leaves joined at the edges. It reminded Ethnic of a dogfish egg case that he once found on a beach. There were several (metal?) objects sandwiched between the two outer cases. The whole effect was a little like vacuum packaging, as if the outside edges had shrunk around the objects they contained.

Two of the objects visible through the casing caught his eye straight away. One was shaped like a skull and a bit of the outer casing over it had worn away revealing what looked like glass just visible inside. The other was a long wide tube around fourteen inches long and with a maybe four inch diameter. This compartment was obviously empty, the casing over it had clearly been cut open and the object prised out.

Alexis was strapping the treasure to the inner frame of the van, 'What happened here?' Ethnic asked pointing to the empty compartment.

'Yes I noticed that, I've no idea, it disappeared the night we lost Nico. We all thought . . .'But Alexis wasn't able to finish.

Back on the bank, the creature was feet away from Red, who was twisting around in her seat frantically searching for Steve. She was right by the second bridge now but the darkness underneath it prevented her from seeing anything.

She stopped shaking the Dal but the noise continued behind her drawing the creature forward and closer to her.

Red panicked, 'Steve . . . STEVE!' she shouted but there was no sign of him. Steve was the most loyal person she'd ever met but now he was gone.

She dropped the Dal into her lap and sat as still as she could as the creature reached her chair and leant over her.
The creatures face was now inches from Red's and Red found herself staring into the creatures eyes. Huge golden eyes swirling, swimming in the moonlight.

The noise from under the bridge came closer, right behind Red now, the creature bobbed its head as it shifted its attention from Red to the source of the sound behind and then back to Red.
Red grabbed the top of the wheels and tried to ease the chair backwards but it bumped into something that prevented it.
The creature's face was inches from Red's but it was looking over her right shoulder.
Not for the first time Red remembered what it had been like to run, all those years ago. She still dreamed about it, could still remember, just pushing her feet into the ground and running, dashing, speeding away, racing away. To leave it all behind and make her world a blur. She still dreamed about it, longed for it but she'd never wanted it as much as this.
The noise was loud now, beside her right ear; Red dragged her eyes from the creatures and turned her head to the right so she could finally see the source of the sound.

A second creature was standing beside and behind her; this creature was bipedal and clearly female but couldn't have been more different. Her skin was covered in bumps and scales like a toad's but the face was that of a woman, not twisted nor grotesque but calm and inquisitive. Her eyes were golden like the first creature but small and human. The skin on her back and on the back of her arms and legs was thicker and heavier, almost like a cloak of scales stuck to her skin. The tymphanium the circular, ear like, disks, rose up from behind her eyes into two semi circular ridges across the top of her head. Moreover she wore clothes or at least her chest, stomach and thighs were covered by a length of bright blue-green fabric twisted around her lithe figure.

The whole effect was spellbinding; Red stared at the creature open mouthed in wonder. She was Neil Armstrong, seeing something that no other human ever had, she stared at the creature in wonder and fascination as it watched her back with equal curiosity and amazement.

The first creature was an animal, an incredible, wonderful marvel of nature but an animal for all that. This second creature was something else entirely, this was no animal. She was human, a different kind of human, a different type of human but she was human, no question, no doubt. Red knew as she looked into her eyes that the mind behind them was at the very least, the equal to her own.

Both creatures now had their faces inches away from Red's and she was captivated by them, she tore her eyes from the eyes of this new creature to look into the eyes of the first, they were mesmerising. As Red stared the world just fell away, she was overcome by a sense of age as if these eyes have been watching the world grow and change for centuries. Her feelings of panic and alarm were long gone now, she knew scientists the world over would have given anything to be where she was right now.

How could she have been so afraid? Why hadn't she

understood?

Then suddenly there was something else, something wonderful, the new creature wanted something, something that she had, something that she could give to her. Red could do something for her; could help her, waves of joy swept over her. She was crying she couldn't help herself and there was only one thing now that she wanted to do.

Red's reached her hands out to both of the creatures; all she wanted to do was to connect with them, was to touch them. As she did so the new creature, the human creature, grabbed both of her hands and folded them into her own.

There was no burning no pain, the first creature reached out also but the second, took her hand, preventing her from touching Red. She knew and understood the danger but was clearly immune herself.

From Ethnic's point of view it only took a second, the grenade landed a few feet from the back of the transit van and exploded immediately. Inside the van the shock wave slammed Ethnic hard against the back of the cab; his foot struck the treasure which they'd just strapped into the corner of the van.

He struggled to pick himself up from the floor; there was another explosion outside and another then shouting and gunfire.

For a moment or two Ethnic lay in the van trying to focus trying to think, it was so bright he couldn't think properly, so loud, so bright then finally he was able to crawl out of the van and fall onto the floor outside.

He dragged himself to his feet as something bounced off the

ground beside him.
'Down - GET DOWN!' Alexis screamed at him as he dived into him and dragged him to the ground just as another explosion rocked the ground nearby.
'What the . . .?'
'Stun grenades keep you head down.'
Ethnic and Alexis were on the humped canal bridge beside the van, the bridge had a wall (waist height) on both sides.
Below the bridge gunfire was coming from both sides of the canal. Alexis was kneeling with the pistol using the wall for cover as bullets ricoched off the side of the bridge. Ethnic was beside Alexis keeping his head down.
'What, who the hell?'
Alexis leapt up and fired five times over the wall, somebody cried out and swore in Russian. 'Andrei's men.'
'They told us they'd got them all!'
Alexis fired again twice, 'They told you that they'd got all of us.' He turned to Ethnic, 'Look they've been stupid they've let me have the higher ground and the van. They're all in front of this bridge your friends are behind it. Go to them, I'll cover you then I'm gone, they'll follow me. Now you go that way – Move.' He pointed to a few steps cut into the end of the wall, Ethnic ran towards them keeping himself as low as he could.
Then two things happened at once.
Firstly the sound of a helicopter came from nowhere as if it had instantly appeared. Then as Ethnic leapt over the steps there was a string of explosions, more stun grenades but not random. This time they *all* went off more or less instantaneously along the tow path either side of the bridge.

One was only yards away from Ethnic and the blast sent him tumbling head over heels into the canal.

As Red reached for the creature's face, it gently pulled away from her. Then there was noise and light, in the distance, shouting and shooting and explosions, both creatures turned away from Red and moved towards the direction of the noise. The older creature moved to the side of the first, bobbing it's heading and hissing softly.

'Red, RED!' Steve was shaking Red. 'C'mon woman, snap out of it.'

'Where were you?' Red gasped.

'Right behind you, I never left you I swear. She was there when I turned round and I couldn't move. I knew you'd be safe, she looked at me and I knew it was okay.' He put his hand on her shoulder. 'I wasn't going to leave you woman, now where the hell is Ethnic and what the bloody hell is going on?' Steve grabbed the handles of the wheelchair and started to drag it back under the bridge.

'No Steve, NO, forward take me forward to them.'

'Are you mad they'll . . .'

'Quickly, trust me Steve quickly.'

Steve hesitated for a second then started pushing the chair along the path to the creatures, they both turned to stare at Steve and Red nervously bobbing their heads.

Red looked at the new creature, 'I know what it is that you want, I know why it is that you've come.'

There were two bright flashes of light, one after the other for a second Red thought it was an explosion, then she realised that Steve has pulled his phone from his pocket and taken a

photo. The creatures and Red stared at Steve.
'Sorry . . .' he spluttered, 'Um I thought a couple of pictures might be nice.'
There was another flash of light but this time it *was* an explosion, a whole series of them. The creatures dropped to the ground pushing their bodies into the long damp grass beside the towpath. Steve toppled over backwards landing half in and half out of the canal. Red's chair tipped over, it felt like she was falling in slow motion. She curled herself up around the Dal and landed hard on the towpath.

Ethnic dragged himself from the canal, the water was freezing and tasted evil, the scene before him was complete pandemonium. The noise from the helicopter was deafening now, the downdraft from the rotors was creating clouds of dust and debris on the bank and shredded branches and twigs were falling from the sky like confetti.
He looked up and right above him he saw the helicopter like a huge black shark in the moonlit sky, ropes hung from its side and men with guns dressed in black were sliding down the ropes shooting at targets on the ground.
Ethnic looked to the bridge and saw Alexis throw his gun over the side and run to the van. Ethnic stared at the van, the doors were still open and the light in the back lit up the whole bridge but the light was shattered and put out for good when the first grenade went off.
Something nagged at his memory, something he saw in that explosion, for an instant, just for a second. There and then he made his mind up, people were everywhere, shooting, shouting and he didn't care, he had to get back into the van

no matter what.

He pulled himself to his feet and raced for the bridge.

There was another bright light, this one from the sky, Ethnic saw a second helicopter high above the first, Ethnic reached the bridge. A man he's not seen before, short and stocky with a thick beard and a pistol was ahead of him, also running toward the van. From nowhere a black garbed figure with a balaclava crashed into the man knocking the gun from his hand. As the force of the impact carried the two of them over the wall of the bridge and down into the canal.

Ethnic didn't care he was almost there, the whole of the van interior was bathed in a bright blue pulsing shimmering light and he was almost there. Then a strong arm grabbed him pulling him back and down to the ground.

'Whoa boyo, keep your head down a minute.' A soldier dressed in black and with a thick welsh accent held onto him firmly. Even with a balaclava Ethnic could see that he was smiling.

The van started to pull away.

'The treasures in there, it's getting away.' Ethnic shouted pointing at the van.

'He's going nowhere mate, now look at me, Jamel look at me, have you got any injuries?'

A second soldier was beside him now then a third, it was like they were appearing out of thin air.

The second helicopter abruptly veered away clearly following the van leaving the first helicopter still hovering low over the canal. Three armed soldiers all clothed in black and wearing balaclavas were kneeling around Ethnic who was lying in a crumpled heap.

'Advise third target acquired, all remaining teams clean up.' The third soldier called calmly into a mic attached to his collar. 'One target on bridge A remaining two at bridge B, landrovers split for pick up.'

'Jamal look at me, any injuries?' the soldier persisted.

'Yeah I'm okay, just wet.' Ethnic spluttered completely bewildered.

'Advise scratches and shock only.' The third soldier said into his mic.

'Jamal look at me, now listen carefully.' The second soldier said firmly. 'This is Alan,' he pointed to the first soldier. 'You and Alan are going to run along the bridge and into that field. Alan will be beside you and he'll keep his hand on your back. Then you're going to run along that hedge till you get to the top of the hill. Do you understand?' Ethnic nodded. 'We will all be with you too, the whole of the way, I'll be in front and Adam here,' he pointed to the remaining soldier, 'will be behind. If one of us say drop you drop to the ground. Do you understand?'

'Yeah top of the hill, drop if you say so, got it.'

'That's no Pontypool accent you from Brum?' Adam asked as calmly as if they were chatting in a pub.

Ethnic nodded.

'City or Villa?'

'Villa.'

'My condolences boyo, right you ready?' Adam looked from Ethnic to the others all who of whom nodded.' Right Leg it!'

With the sound of gunfire still ringing around them, they ran off together along the bridge.

Red was lying across the canal towpath clearly shaken, it took her a few moments to catch her breath and orientate herself. The wheelchair was on its side on the edge of the canal. One of the back wheels was badly buckled. Steve was dragging himself to his feet and shaking his head.
'Stun grenades, it's okay they're just stun grenades and my phone's waterproof,' he mumbled still dazed but on his feet now. 'They're just meant to disorientate that's all.' He said as he turned around and walked straight back into the canal.
The creatures raised themselves from the grass, their heads bobbing nervously. Red looked around her frantically, she saw the Dal on the towpath a few feet away and crawled toward it. 'Here I've got it.' She grabbed it and held it out to the new creature, 'this is what you came for isn't it?'
The new creature leapt forward and squatted beside Red, slowly and carefully it took the Dal from her hand.
There was a sudden noise overhead; Red knew it was a helicopter, very low and very close.
'Go quickly, this place is no longer safe for you, GO!' Red told the creature's urgently. For a moment both creatures stared back at her, she felt that they were looking into her soul, that they could see every hope, every dream and every fear. Then in a heartbeat they were gone leaping into the black canal and disappearing beneath its restless surface.
Steve crawled out of the canal and over to Red. 'Can we just stick to school treasure hunts from now on?'
Before Red could answer two soldiers dressed head to foot in black appeared running down the bank towards them.
The first soldier dropped to his knees beside Red and Steve, the second knelt in front of them, his back to them,

automatic rifle raised watching back along the bank.

'Evening gorgeous,' the first soldier smiled through his balaclava. 'My name's Ben and that's Bill by there. Are you injured?'

'You're not really Bill and Ben are you?'Red answered.

The soldier laughed loudly, 'Ben and Bill will do for now, are you hurt Jenifer?'

'Advise *two* targets at B - nearest team please,' Bill called calmly into his mic.

'I'm fine honestly,' Red replied, 'Never better.'

The soldier turned to Steve, 'Eli, look at me, are you injured?'

'I'm fine, we're both fine but our friend is over there in the middle of that.' Steve pointed to what appeared to be a minor war zone in the distance.

'Advise on Jamel' Bill called into his mic, then after a moment he replied, 'Roger. - He's okay our colleagues are extracting him now.' He told them without taking his eyes from the path.

Two more soldiers appeared running along the bank and dropped down beside the others. One joined Bill knelt beside him gun raised watching the bank, the other knelt beside Steve.

'Ok now this is what we're going to do, we're all going on a little moonlit run,' Ben told them matter of factly. 'Jenifer I'll carry you, Eli this is Keith (Keith nodded) he's going to run alongside you with Ken (the fourth soldier nodded without taking his eye from the gun-sight.) Keith will keep his hand on your back and he'll guide you cos it's hard to see and we need you to keep your head down. If anyone says drop you drop to the ground.'

'Ken and Keith?' Red and Steve questioned together, their evening becoming more surreal with each passing minute. The two soldiers grinned hugely back at them through their balaclava's.

'Will be behind and in front providing cover.' Ben continued.

'How did you know we were . . .' Steve began.

'Time for that later. Our job now is to get you out safely. Now you ready?'

Red and Steve nodded.

'Right Sweetie,' Ben scooped up Red like she was weightless, 'Arms round my neck and hold on tight.' He turned to the others, 'Ready? - GO!'

Together they ran off into the night.

Eight

Red and the boys (all covered in mud and looking pale and shattered) were sat in a large plain office room with a big rectangular mirror on the wall. The Police station was a scene of chaos; two officers were talking on the phone, one to Nevill Hall Hospital, one to the South Wales Argus, both were shouting, trying to make their voices heard over the racket in the room. Half a dozen uniformed officers and three plain clothed 'seniors' were pretty much all talking at once. The whole scene was one of complete disorganisation, with people entering and leaving the room. The tall young policeman Red met at the school strode angrily towards Red and the boys, the three of them looked shell-shocked.

Stood against the far wall was a man who clearly wasn't a police officer. He was in his late fifties, immaculate dark three piece suit, collar and tie. He had a receding hairline and looked tired. He had been wordlessly watching proceedings and was clearly not happy.

The tall young policeman rounded on the youngsters, 'Why's it always you three?' he snapped.

'Neither warranted nor appropriate officer, get out!' the man shouted glaring at the young policeman (who left quickly). The man caught Red's eye as he slowly and deliberately drew out and checked a pocket watch from his waistcoat chest pocket (despite the presence of a large clock on the wall next to him.) Red recognised the watch at once and acted immediately.

She slammed both of her hands down on the tabletop in front of her as hard as she could and shouted 'Enough!' at

the top of her voice.
Everyone else in the room (apart from the man in the suit) jumped and turned to look at her. 'Two of us are minors; we've been kidnapped at gun point and dragged into a bloody war zone. The three of us are soaked and not one of you has even offered us a towel. We're freezing to death and you can't even give us a cup of tea!'
The whole room fell silent, everyone staring at Red.
'Everybody out except him! 'Red demanded pointing to the man in the suit. 'We're not talking to anyone except him!'
The man stepped forward into the middle of the room, 'I think Jenifer's made herself quiet clear, now leave us.'
Two of the senior plain-clothed officers looked accusingly at the man but they all started reluctantly to leave. The man in the suit pulled a notebook with a pencil banded to it from his pocket, he scribbled onto a sheet which he removed and handed to the oldest plain clothed officer. 'These two are on their way here with the parents, the moment they arrive they'll all be brought to that large room at the end of the corridor, we'll be in there.'
'Now just a moment, that room's our . . .' one of the senior officers began.
'We'll be in there,' the man cut in ignoring his objection completely. 'Now I asked one of your officers to bring a wheelchair here seven minutes ago, I know you've got three of them on site, go and find out what's keeping them and organise some tea and towels.
The officer left sheepishly, whilst the man in the suit gestured to the three of them to stay silent.
Ethnic turned to Red, 'We've just spent the night in the

Twilight Zone and all you can think to ask them for is a cup of tea and a towel? - I mean seriously a cup of tea and a towel! - you're meant to be the brains of the outfit.'

'I do like a nice cup of tea mind!' Steve cut in.

The Man in the suit was smiling (despite himself.)

'Who is this guy?' Ethnic whispered.

'Jenifer recognised my watch,' he drew it out of his pocket so that Ethnic could see it.

'Hey that's the same as . . .'

'Samantha's yes.'

A WPC entered the room with a wheelchair and some towels, 'Jenifer we can't find your Mum, is she out? Do you know where she is ?' she asked as Steve and Ethnic helped Red into the chair.

'She's out of the country, don't worry I'll send her a text and my aunt's coming round later.' Red lied, she'd never hear the end of it if her Mum found out.

They followed the man to the room at the end of the corridor.

They entered the room and made themselves comfortable; a CSO arrived with a tray laden with tea, a small pot of milk and bowl of sugar as well as biscuits and crisps. Malcolm took the tray and set it carefully on a table in the middle of the room. 'Now shall I be mother? - Milk and Sugar?' he asked looking up to them.

'White two please.' Red said.

'Black three please.' Steve said.

'White four please.' Ethnic said.

Malcolm stared at Ethnic for a moment, then complied.

'Samantha and your headmaster are on their way but I

suspect with all the excitement outside it might take them a while.' He told them as he passed them their tea.

'What with World War three starting on the Monmouthshire canal.' Ethnic observed.

'Hardly World War Three, more a small skirmish between special-forces and an armed terrorist cell looking to hide a few weapons in rural Monmouthshire.'

'Skirmish, a few weapons!' Ethnic protested, '- there were helicopters and . . .'

The man silenced him with a raised hand.

'Who are you?' Red asked him coolly.

'My name is Malcolm Morris.'

'Of . . .'

'Well let me see GCHQ, MI5, MI6 which would you like?'

'Which is it?'

'Maybe one of them, maybe none of them. It doesn't matter, it won't help.

'No? - well I've a question for you Mr Malcolm Morris,' Ethnic cut in, 'What the bloody hell is going on?'

'We understood that the Major's - Samantha's office had been disbanded.' Red added.

'Allow me to explain and answer both of your questions.' He pointed to the tray gesturing for them to help themselves. Steve and Ethnic needed no further encouragement.

'That PCSO who just brought the tea start's her shift tomorrow morning, she goes into town and everyone can see that she's there.' Malcolm was making himself a cup now, black no sugar. 'The first woman that she meets and talks to is concerned about her neighbour, she doesn't know what, if anything , she should do, so she talks to the PCSO.' Malcolm settled himself down in an armchair opposite Red and the boys. 'The PCSO then radios that information to colleagues who are in the neighbour's area. Twenty minutes later those colleagues will break the neighbour's door down after they look through the letterbox and see that the woman is unconscious on the floor. The ambulance they call will save the neighbours life.'

Malcolm took a sip of his tea, 'Across the road from the PCSO is an addict in a car, he's desperate to get cash for a fix and the newsagent he's parked outside has just got one old guy on the till. He's ready to rob it then he sees the PCSO, he panics and leaves. Had he tried to rob it, the old guy on the till would have had a heart attack in the scuffle but that's prevented. It's not Ten AM yet but the PCSO has already saved two lives. But nobody knows, there's no proof, no stats, no positive outcomes. The PCSO's presence prevents and protects but it can't be quantified as there's no evidence.'

Red nodded.

'Politicians want to prove that they're getting things done, want to point to facts and figures but there are types of work that are unable to prove what they achieve because what they achieve is prevention. They can't prove what's been prevented because what's been prevented hasn't happened. So there are no facts nor figures no proof. Samantha's department was about prevention, what happened tonight happened because it wasn't prevented when it would have been in the past.'

'Cutbacks?' Red asked him quietly.

'Indeed cutbacks he said with a wry smile, he turned to Ethnic. 'When things happen that haven't been prevented, it's my job to manage and end that event.'

'Event?!'

'How else would you describe it?'

'Do you know, I think my original description world war three came pretty close.' Ethnic told him, 'It was like a Metallica concert down there.'

'Indeed, I am sure from your point of view it wasn't a quiet evening.'

'Wasn't a quiet evening!?' Ethnic gasped.

'Mr Morris what happened to Alexis? And who's got the treasure?' Red asked.

'How did you know we were there? It would have been gunfire in the dark but the soldiers knew that we were there and they were looking for us.' Steve added.

Malcolm smiled, 'No you don't disappoint do you,' he told the three of them. 'Yes the soldiers were there looking for you, shall I start from the beginning?'

'Please.'

'Samantha is nobody's fool, if she thinks something's going on then something is almost certainly going on. She and Harold got the police involved as soon as you'd found the information in the house at Usk.'

Ethnic was on his feet in an instant. 'Y'see Harold Williams is in on it as well he's in some secret government spy thing with the Major.'

They're both in the same Bridge group,' Malcolm said dryly, 'Meet at Llanover once a month.' Ethnic slumped back in his chair, 'Samantha had to include him. Three of his pupils, two of whom are minors get themselves involved with rival international treasure hunters one of whom had already been killed. Of course she got the police involved and of course she kept your headmaster in the loop and of course she got *me* involved. The Romanians and the Russians were easily rounded up, a little too easily we thought. Samantha was concerned that you'd either get dragged back in or that temptation would get the better of you. So we put a tracker on your car.'

Ethnic was back on his feet and properly outraged. 'What, you put a . . . on my . . . on our . . . isn't this just what I've always been saying, this government is secretly watching everyone. I bet you hacked our computers as well?'

Oh please, why does your generation think that the government's secretly listening in to what you're thinking and saying when you're all so eager to plaster every thought and notion that you ever have all over social media.'

Malcolm replied dismissively, 'My god have you ever looked at twitter, it's the word banal given life. You think that intelligence officers want to spend their lives wading through the tedious self-important dross that most people feel that the world demands that they share online?' He took another brisk sip of his tea. 'A year ago we were tracking somebody of 'interest' to us on social media. The concern was that he was sharing coded information with agents abroad using his twitter account, in plain sight as it were. We read through it, waded through it. Every thought he had, every decision he made, what he had for breakfast, what he wore to work, what the traffic was like. Page after page, day after day, there had to be something there, something hidden, some code, nobody could really think any of this mattered surely. Nobody would really take the time to write all of this down. Nobody could think anyone else could possibly want to read it all. There had to be something hidden, we were so sure. You know what we found?'

The three of them shook their heads and Ethnic sat back down.

Nothing! There was nothing there, nothing to find. It really was what it was, he had *forty seven* followers. I swear three security assistants in my department pretty much lost the will to live wading through his life online. You think the government wants to know what people are typing into their computers? Have a really good look, look properly, look objectively at twitter or facebook then ask yourself - would you?'

He stopped as his phone beeped; he scanned it for a second before dropping it back into his pocket. 'We put a tracker on your car, you went into Raglan services at seven fifteen pm and were still there at nine thirty. They stop serving food at eight so we were concerned. We checked the location of your phones . . .'

'You put trackers on our phones too?' Ethnic was on his feet again.

'The three of you have modern GPS enabled Smart phones which have trackers built in, in case the phone is stolen.' He told Ethnic wearily.

'But you'd have needed our passwords.' Red pointed out.

'We could have gone to the providers direct but this takes time, our operators will usually try a couple of old favourites first. The word password is the first we try and it turns out that password is the password that one of you was using.' Ethnic suddenly looked uncomfortable and sank back into his chair.

'The moment we found out that the three of you were beside the canal in the middle of nowhere whilst your vehicle was still at the services, well let's put it this way, things hit the fan.' Malcolm continued. 'We had a 'team' on stand-by then a treble nine comes in automatic gunfire location, Monmouthshire canal a few miles from Abergavenny. Not a shotgun, automatic gunfire in the same location as your phones and at that point its gloves off and you three are our first priority. Our team are based in Brecon and were already in the air and on the way to Raglan; it took them two minutes to divert to you and another four to extract you.'

Malcolm took another sip of tea then smiled at Red. 'You put our sniper in a real predicament, he's in the chopper as his mates go over the side and he's there with an infrared gun sight. He's been ordered to take the creature if it gets close enough to touch one of you but the creatures are cold-blooded and he can barely see them. Fortunately it takes a few moments for their bodies to equilibrate with their surroundings every time that they move. Our modern gun sights are very accurate *and* yes Jenifer we know that there were two of them.' He paused for a moment, his eyes holding Red's. 'If you want the whole truth to come out you must first ask yourself this question. What will happen to the creatures if people know that they are real and know where they are?'

Red looked at the boys then back to Malcolm Morris. 'They didn't want to hurt me, the old one, she, she got into my head. She was right by me and stopped the smaller one touching me but all she wanted was for me to give her the Dal.'

'Dal?' Malcolm looked blank.

'It's what the Romanians called the Bell.'

Malcolm was visibly surprised, 'She's got the bell?'

'She took it out of my hands, really carefully, so gently like she was afraid of hurting me. I knew she wanted it and I just wanted her to have it. It was like I couldn't help myself. I'm sorry.'

Malcolm shook his head, 'No, no don't worry. This is unexpected I had assumed it was at the bottom of the canal.'

'Why would the creature want the bell?' Ethnic asked.

'Why wouldn't she, the bell was control and somehow she understood that.' Malcolm mused staring into the distance. 'This is clearly something that we've underestimated. They are far more intelligent than we allowed for.'

He finished his Tea and carefully returned his cup to the tray. 'If the media get hold of this, it will become a circus. It will begin with the greatest scientific discovery of the age and end with poisonous monsters in every shadow threatening our very existence. The creatures will have to be caught and contained, to keep the public safe you understand. They'll be put on exhibit, examined, dissected, and shared with the world.'

Red looked at the boys and then back to Malcolm, 'That's not what we want.'

'I know and neither do I,' Malcolm smiled, 'We'll stick with the chemical suit for now.'

'What about the treasure?' Steve asked.

'The helicopter reached your location lights out. Jenifer was easy to spot and not in immediate danger. The officer who's covering her can see two targets through the infrared, not human and like ghosts but they're moving away from Jenifer and they disappear into the canal. In the water their bodies equilibrate in seconds so they're invisible. The infrared shows us a tight group of figures and there's clearly gunfire. Two of the figures on the ground are identified as carrying and using automatic weapons so these are taken by snipers in the helicopter immediately. The remaining officers go over the side using ropes to get to the ground. On the ground they work in pairs. We already know where Jenifer is so one pair goes for her, the first officer will carry her out whist his companion provides cover. Luck is on their side as when they reach her, (he points at Steve) you're there too. All the officers wear a mic the first pair call a second pair to extricate the two of you, two officers guide and carry, their companions cover you, and them, as they do so.'

Malcolm paused for questions but the youngsters just gestured for him to continue. He turned and pointed at Ethnic. 'That leaves you, the officers aboard the helicopter can now see one of the remaining traces is - erm - a little smaller than the others.'

Red and Steve smirked much to Ethnic's annoyance.

'Two offices head for this trace and find you trying to get into the back of a Ford transit.'

'I told them the treasure was in there but they dragged me away.'

'Their first priority was to get you out in one piece. This they did and the second that the three of you were safe, all the remaining teams on the ground have only one other task.

'Which was?'
'Not too hard to work out what that was surely?' Malcolm said to Steve dryly. 'Their primary function was to locate and extricate. Once this is achieved then their job then is to remove the threat on the ground as quickly and cleanly as possible. Minimum casualties obviously but you have to understand the scene was chaotic, one officer said it was like the wild-west.'
'You're telling me!' Ethnic agreed.
'What happened to Alexis?' Red asked.
'Whilst Jamel was being dragged from the back of the transit, your man Alexis the last Romanian got into the front and drove it away. The officers in the helicopter couldn't leave the scene as they were controlling the action on the ground but there was another helicopter on the scene, a Police helicopter. This followed the van and called for a police road unit to stop the van with a stinger which was done. The driver managed to escape but the van was recovered. There was nothing in the back of the van.'
'It was there, definitely, I helped him put it in there.' Ethnic protested.
'We know, the back doors of the van were open when it pulled off. Two officers saw the contents and it was there and it was strapped down when the van pulled away. The helicopter had eyes on the van from the moment that it left the canal to the moment that it skidded off the road after hitting the stinger. Nobody was in the back, the van didn't stop and nothing fell out of the back but when the van was stopped the treasure was gone.
Ethnic stared at Malcolm open-mouthed, 'Alexis must have

had it.' Red suggested.
'No, he was chased by two police officers on foot, he wasn't carrying anything. He only escaped because he ran onto a disused office site at Mamhilad and through a gate which locked when he pulled it shut behind him. The officers had to climb a fence to get to him by which time he'd gone.'
Ethnic thought for a moment, 'Police helicopters have infrared though couldn't they track him?'
'As soon as the van crashed the helicopter returned to the canal, several of the Russians were casualties and we needed to get them to Nevill Hall. Now what I need from you three is a full statement of everything that Alexis told you about the creature and the treasure. Oh and we'll need the photo's that Eli's taken on the phone in the back pocket of his jeans.'
Before Steve could answer, a soldier entered the room still wearing the black trousers but with a different jacket and no Balaclava. He winked at Red who instantly recognised his bright blue eyes. 'You alright gorgeous?' he asked.
Malcolm sighed and rolled his eyes, 'Time and place James.'
'James is it?' Red asked him. He grinned at her as he handed Malcolm a small electronic tablet, Malcolm frowned at the screen.
'Thought as much, the paperwork's going to be horrendous. Are you *all* alright?' he asked him handing back the tablet.
'Two light shrapnel, one bullet in the calf and Douglas dislocated his shoulder taking one of them over the bridge.'
Malcolm winced.
'It's okay we popped it back in for him on the bank.'

'I'm sure he appreciated that.'

'Afterwards, yes.'

'Was anyone killed?' Red asked.

Malcolm and the soldier exchanged glances.

'They weren't soldiers but when we arrived we didn't know that. There was gunfire from half a dozen or so on the ground and two of them were firing machine pistols. We couldn't take any chances.'

'So that's another two.'

'Another two?' Malcolm questioned raising one eyebrow.'

'Look I've got to scoot,' James interrupted as he turned to leave' 'Bye sweetie.'

'Bye James,' Red blushed.

Steve and Ethnic turned to each other and both pretend to vomit.

'Another two?' Malcolm repeated.

'There's four more buried beside the bridge.' Steve told him.

Malcolm rolled his eyes, 'James' he said just as James was reaching for the door.'

'Three more Romanians and a local Pensioner.' Red added.

'Oh this just keeps on getting better,' Malcolm moaned sarcastically.

'Want me to tell group?' James asked waiting at the door.

'No it's recovery I'll organise but . . .'

'You don't want anymore . . .'

'I don't want *anything* else disappearing. No.' Malcolm

interrupted pointedly eyeing the youngsters

'I'll get a couple of lads down there to keep an eye on things then.' James turned and left the room.

Malcolm turned back to them, 'Now you three, I need you to tell me everything.'

Nine

Niki Meadows was beginning to hate Africa; she admitted it to herself as she clambered into the projects battered rusty landrover. The vehicle was parked barely a hundred yards away from where she was camped but three days of rain had turned the whole site into a quagmire. She'd been reasonably presentable when she'd left her tent, she'd managed to wash her hair and she'd managed to find a top that although clearly not recently cleaned and pressed, was at least tidy enough for a video call. The journey from the tent though had caused her to slip and fall three times and despite the soft ground she'd managed to twist her ankle as well as getting herself plastered in the slimy, sticky mud that the region was known for.

She'd had the good sense to bag her laptop and notes so they were at least intact; she peered into the rear view mirror frowning at the sight, then laughed at herself. She did, at least now, look every inch the field biologist.

After several twists of the key the coughing engine finally burst into life and Niki was driving towards what was laughingly called the main road.

The position in Africa had sounded so appealing, so exotic, she'd been so excited, looked forward to it so much but the truth was, that now that she was here, she was just bored and frustrated.

She carefully steered the landrover around the putrid remains of a five day dead Hippo lying in the road. The smell was truly awful and stayed with her for nearly quarter of a mile. If she was being honest it wasn't the place she told herself, nor the people, on the contrary they were all welcoming and fun to work with. It was the work itself that was the problem or more to the point, it was the subjects.

To an Amphibian specialist about the only claim to fame that Hymenochirus possessed was that they were first bred in captivity by Ken Livingstone. They were quite interesting little frogs in their own right, completely aquatic and, and well that was it really. Niki had spent months with them; there was a considerable amount of un-regulated mining in the area which resulted in all sorts of chemicals getting into the rivers. These chemicals in turn found their way into the organisms that lived in the rivers. So these little aquatic frogs became barometers of their waterways, by analysing them you could get a feeling for what was going on in their environment.

Nothing wrong with any of that except this was Africa and there were some really cool, really exciting, really interesting frogs in Africa.

Pyxicephalus wandered around the camp like extras from a Tim Burton movie and Conraua the size of rabbits weren't that far away. There were fascinating, jaw-dropping amphibians all around, creatures that demanded attention, demanded to be studied.

Niki Meadows had left her home In England to travel half way round the world to the home of some of the most fascinating Amphibians that an enthusiast could encounter. Having done this she was spending all her time and devoting all of her effort to collecting and studying tiny little frogs that you could buy for £3.99 each in the tropical fish shop next door to her house in Bristol.

After three hours of driving she reached Kinshasa and eventually found the Embassy. The man on the gate seemed to be expecting her and waved her in with a huge smile. She parked next to another landrover near the main entrance and was met by a secretary named Ruth who lead her into a large spacious lounge.

'Take a seat and let me get you a drink, what would you like?' the secretary asked with another flashing smile.

'Anything cold please.'

The secretary grinned and walked over to a large cabinet. She returned after a moment with a tall glass of lemonade which boasted a slice of lemon and half a dozen ice cubes.

'Mr Phillips will be with you in a minute.' She told her handing her the glass.

'Thank you so much, that is *most* welcome,' Niki told her sincerely. 'Is Mr Phillips the Ambassador?'

'No, one of his assistants.' Ruth replied and before she could elaborate, the Mr Phillips in question came into the room.

'Miss Meadows?' he offered her his hand but his eyes wandered over her boots and hair.

She stood and took his hand to shake it, suddenly aware of how clean the room was and how muddy she was. 'I apologise for my appearance but I *was* summoned from the field,' she told him.

'Quite,' Mr Phillips replied with a raised eyebrow. 'The office is upstairs, might I ask you to take your boots off.'

Niki sat back down to remove her boots and then her socks which she discovered were equally plastered.

'Ruth do you think you could-' he glanced from the boots to the secretary. 'This way Miss Fields.'

'That's Meadows she told him as she followed him through one door whilst Ruth carried her boots and socks at arms length out of the other.

Niki followed him from the room into a large ornate hall which had a white stone floor, wonderfully cool to her bare feet and up a broad spiral staircase which reminded her of how sore her ankle still was. 'Can you tell me what all of this is about? – the university doesn't normally go to these lengths to get in touch,' she asked.

'I can't tell you what this is all about but I can tell you that it's not a university that wants to talk to you.'

'Not the university? – then who?'

'London.'

'London! Who in London? – I don't know anybody in London.'

'The call is from London Miss Fields, that's all I know.'

'That's Meadows,' she reminded him as they trudged on up the staircase.

'Oh bugger!' they'd just reached the top of the staircase when Niki remembered, 'I've left my laptop and notes in the landrover.'

'They'll be quite safe.'

'That wasn't what I was worried about, I'll need them for the call.'

'You won't need anything for the call, you didn't need to bring anything with you.' He pushed open one of the dark wooden doors at the top of the staircase and lead her into a small plush office room.

In the centre of the room was an elaborate wooden table bearing a large computer monitor with a keyboard in front of it. A telephone receiver was plugged into the keyboard where the mouse would have been.

Mr Phillips pointed to the keyboard which had an additional number pad with several coloured keys, 'Just press that green key when I leave the room Miss Field's and the Red when you finish the call.'

'That's Meadows,' she told him as he left the room.

Niki Meadows sat down and stared at the lifeless monitor, she regretted leaving her drink on the table downstairs as her mouth was suddenly very dry. This was all completely surreal; she knew nothing was wrong at home as she'd spoken to her Mother and Brother via Facebook the day before, when she'd first been told about the call. She knew nobody in London and all of this cloak and dagger stuff was bizarre but there was, now at least, one way to find out. She raised the receiver to her ear and pressed the green button, she had no idea that her life was about to change forever. There was a ringing tone for a few seconds, 'Miss Meadows I presume,' said the voice in old school English, 'hold on a moment.' Abruptly the monitor came to life and a man's head and shoulders slowly came into focus. He was in his late fifties, had a receding hairline and was smartly dressed.
'I see you've come from the field.' He said the faintest of smiles pulling at the corners of his mouth.
'I've driven for four hours through a deluge to get here,' she exaggerated effortlessly. 'Mr-?'
'Morris, Malcolm Morris.'
'Mr Malcolm Morris of?'
'That's on a need to know basis i'm afraid and at the moment you don't need to know.'
'At this moment I don't *need* to take this phone call.'
'Ok then, bye.'

Niki paused, she knew all she had to do was press the Red button, problem was then she wouldn't know. She would hate not knowing.

'Ok then, you tell me what this is about.'

'Ten years ago a Fossil was discovered in the American badlands that was classified as coming from an unknown species of Raptor. You felt that the classification was incorrect and that the Fossil represented something quite different. You wrote an essay on the subject and were pilloried for it.'

Niki's heart sank, the backlash that essay had caused pretty much wrecked her career; she'd been ridiculed and mocked by the community that she loved. Even now, years later, spiteful remarks and comments were still fired in her direction on a regular basis. Despite, or maybe because of, all the cloak and dagger nonsense she'd been secretly quite excited about taking this call, now it was *this* again. 'I feel I've said all I can on that subject, everybody has a right to interpret-'

'Miss Meadows.'

'If scientists are not prepared to keep an open mind, then-'

'Miss Meadows.'

'What is the point of-'

'Miss Meadows, I spend a lot of my time talking to and in the company of, Politicians. Let me tell you about politicians, apart from one or two very rare exceptions, they are not real.

Everything they think, do and say is weighed, measured and calculated to achieve only what they desire for themselves and to satisfy their own internal agenda's. None can think more than four years ahead.

Malcolm paused, 'It is for me a very real and totally genuine pleasure to talk to a passionate, caring and genuine person such as yourself and if I may say so the mud in your hair and the sweat on your brow do you more credit than any salon hairstyle or any amount of makeup ever could. It would be a real pleasure to bandy words with you all night but it's four in the morning here and I need to know if you will leave your little puddle frogs and come back to the United kingdom to do the job you were born to do.'

Niki stared back at him open mouthed.

'If you accept the position, you'll be a scientific advisor based in Whitehall answerable to me alone; you'll have an office and the use of a secretary or a p.a. should you require one. I'll even put a little tank with some Hymenochirus in the corner for you. However most of the time you'll be working in the field. Clear so far?'

'What no, wait I don't understand what?'

'Good let me show you your subjects. The reason that you've had to drive across Africa for *three hours* is because this line is secure and you are about to find out why that is so important. Are you sitting comfortably?' Malcolm gave her his best smile.

Niki nodded lost for words.
'The piece of film you will see first was shot with an infrared camera on board a special forces helicopter. The section you will be watching has been enhanced because the creatures are cold blooded so they barely registered on the first print. The two still photographs that follow were taken by a remarkable young man a few moments before on the ground. You will tell nobody about the film or the photographs do I make myself clear?

Niki nodded, then Niki watched and it was then that Niki knew that her life had changed forever.

After the film and after the photo's, Malcolm's face reappeared on the screen as Niki sat there crying like a baby.

His face by contrast was calmness itself, his voice barely a whisper. 'Are you interested?'

It took a moment or two for her to regain her composure, 'I'm yours,' she told him.

A week later and there was still a police presence at the school. Red and the boys had told them everything that Malcolm had told them to and over the next few days the Police searched the Library, the chemistry labs and the sports sheds.

They didn't appear to have found anything but from Red and the boys point of view the information exchange only seemed to work in one direction. What made matters worse was that nobody would leave them alone. Suddenly everybody wanted to talk and know what they were doing and what they were up to, so they had had little chance to talk together and reflect.

This was hard on Steve in particular who needed time on his own and time alone with Red and Ethnic to absorb and digest the events of that night.

In the end they had to resort to drastic measures to be able to go somewhere to talk where nobody could spy on them. There was a music storeroom at the back of the school which was the only part of the school that didn't have (and needed) a ramp. It was intended to be a storage area for the cleaners but it had been pinched by the ever growing music department. Steve had signed out the key earlier. Now he and Ethnic were slowly and carefully carrying Red up the narrow concrete staircase.

Progress was slow.

'Do you reckon if we put her in a straight jacket?' Steve said to Ethnic.

'Yeah and tie her to the back of the chair that might keep her still for a moment.'

'I'm trying to sit still but you've got me at a stupid angle, what am I supposed to hold onto?'

'No appreciation, I notice you didn't complain when *James* carried you.' Ethnic pointed out.

'James was an expert! - James was a professional!'

'James didn't have to carry you upstairs and James didn't carry your chair. Sit still woman.' Steve told her.

'How can I sit still with you two? – it's like the Chuckle brothers trying to move a piano.'

'To me,' Ethnic chuckled.

'To you,' Steve laughed back.

'Oh God.'

They reached the top and carefully placed her down. Both Steve and Ethnic paused to catch their breath.

'If you'd just keep still woman, it would be so much easier.' Steve panted.

At that point Peter the sixteen year old who'd just transferred that year was walking past them to go down the stairs and had heard their banter.

'Yeah you need to learn to keep still woman,' he said to Red. 'You won't bounce if you're dropped.'

Steve grabbed Peter by the collar and rammed him firmly

into the wall behind him. 'You're new so this'll just be warning. Me and him,' his eyes flicked to Ethnic, 'are her mates. Got it?' Steve told him firmly his face inches away from Peter's.

Peter nodded sheepishly.

'We can talk to her like that but you can't, got it?'

'I only meant . . .' Peter started.

'Bye then.' Ethnic said.

Peter left quickly.

'Guys . . . he didn't –'

'Not the point!' Steve replied pushing the key into the storeroom door and opening it.

'I'm sure they're watching us.' Ethnic said looking round the room as they went in.

The dark untidy room was dusty and full of instruments of all types just piled up on each other. Not in here they're not.' Red assured him.

Steve grabbed two chairs from a stack and placed them in the middle of the room facing Red. 'Ok then – Now what?'

Ethnic dropped into the chair beside him, 'Yeah – what do we do now?'

'What can we do now?' Red threw her hands up. 'The creatures will be okay, I'm sure of that.'

'Yeah but what about the treasure?' Ethnic moaned.

'Police and special-forces have combed every inch of every place that van went and found nothing.' Red reminded him,

'Where do we even start?'
Ethnic wasn't impressed, 'So we just give up?'
'I'm not saying we give up – I'm just saying that at the moment there's very little that we can do.'
The three of them sat silently and glumly in the cluttered little room for a few moments.
'It's not that that's bugging me though.'
Both boys looked at her questioningly.
'I just can't shake the feeling that we're missing something, 'she told them quietly.
They soon left the room as they couldn't have it for long and Steve had to return the key. It was final lesson time now and another school day would soon be over.

The school within an hour or so fell quiet; a place that had been so loud and alive was now silent and empty.
Old Stan the caretaker, long past retirement age and seemingly part of the school's fixtures and fittings made his way around the deserted school buildings to lock up after the cleaners. It was dark outside now and yet more rain pelted the roof and windows, as Stan finished his round.
He made his way down the long corridor towards the school's main entrance. Past the long rows of Lockers with brightly painted doors now different shades of grey in the darkened building. Now if Stan had been a younger man, he might have seen it, he might have noticed.

An eerie pulsing blue light was visible through the keyhole of one of the lockers, that locker was Jenifer's.

Extracts from 'Jenifer and the Lost: The Witch's Kiss'

Christopher Rudd walked the short distance between his vicarage at the bottom of the village and his church, St Catherine's at the top. On a Thursday, he told himself with a smile despite his headache, Marysfield was the *village* that time forgot.

He'd spent the previous evening with Arthur Conan Doyle and a bottle of red, the one advantage of a dwindling congregation was that he now had more time to himself in the evenings. That combined with having his three kids in three different uni's meant time to himself was no longer the luxury it had been.

He found that the slight hill was causing him to pant a little more than usual, he wasn't getting the exercise he'd been used to either. Maybe he should join a Gym or give up the red; he considered this for a moment and decided it wouldn't pay to rush into anything. He had after all; plenty of time and the headache prevented him from wanting to think too much about anything.

He reached the top of the hill and his church and glanced idly over the wall, what he saw turned him cold.

A long narrow graveyard lay behind the church; it was crowded and cluttered with statues and headstones. Beside the graveyard lay another long strip of land, about half the length of a football field (and often used as one by the youth club). The land was left undeveloped, it was owned by the church, even included in the original deeds but included

with the strict condition that the land was *never* to be developed or even dug over.
This actually wasn't a problem as Christopher had soon discovered. The EU made money available in the form of grants to encourage landowners to leave strips of land fallow to encourage and sustain wildlife.
This meant that the church was paid to basically leave this ground alone, it wasn't a great amount but these days every little helped. This suited the church as they couldn't legally touch the land nor do anything with it. Furthermore the land was useless anyway, it wasn't suitable for development and nothing would grow there, anything planted there just died. A patchy, wiry, yellow grass covered the ground but even that never grew long enough to warrant cutting and as for encouraging wildlife. Nothing would go anywhere near it.
This morning however something was indeed happening on the land.
Seven people were stood waist deep in a large hole that they were digging in the middle of the ground. The diggers were just about the most incongruous group imaginable, five men and two women. Two of the men wore expensive suits, another was a policeman in full uniform, Christopher recognised Tom the landlord of the Rat and Ferret and Mike a local skinhead. The one woman smartly dressed, hair in a bun, he knew was a teacher at the nearby primary. The other, the oldest of the group, was Grace Williams a local

pensioner who Christopher knew well and had expected to meet inside the church that morning. She came in on Thursdays to do the flowers. Grace was frail and waiting for a hip transplant, here she was up to her knees in soil, swinging a Pickaxe.

'What are you doing?' Christopher spluttered, his head suddenly pounding. 'Grace, Tom, what in the world?'

The group ignored him intent on their labour, in an instant he was running for the front of the church where he flung the old wrought iron gate open and raced around to the graveyard.

Grace William's waist deep in soil, face speckled with sweat and mud grinned hugely to him as he ran towards the, now, large hole behind the gravestones. 'Good morning Vicar,' she chirped, her voice unusually strong. The rest of the group just carried on digging as if it was the most normal thing in the world.

'Grace what?' Christopher stammered his eyes sweeping in the scale of the excavation, 'What in the blazes is going on here?' he panted.

'Better ask the boss' Grace grinned back at him nodding over his shoulder.

Christopher span around and for the second time that morning what he saw turned him cold.

An hour and twenty minutes later Malcolm pulled up in the car park at the back of the old hospital where the elderly victim had been sectioned. The young woman was waiting by the entrance, there was nothing unusual about her appearance now. She wore a white doctor's tunic over a plain black dress, a photo-card id hung from a lanyard around her neck and her injured hand was invisible in one of the tunic pockets. Malcolm climbed from his car and walked to her, his eyes on her shoulders.

'They're still there, they're part of me, it's just you can't see, look closely.' She said following his gaze.

As he stared Malcolm thought he saw a slight shimmer in the air behind her head, like cold air over a hot car bonnet in the sun.

'You see no illusion is really perfect, once you know something's there and you're looking for it the eye becomes harder to fool. If you looked for long enough and concentrated hard enough you'd see. If people don't expect to see anything then they won't.' She told him.

They walked into the building and up to a locked door with a keypad and bell. She pressed the bell and hissed 'leave this to me to Malcolm.' As a nurse in a dark blue uniform opened the door.

'Doctor Joanne Smith, you are expecting me and this is Mr Malcolm Morris whose department is overseeing the police investigation.'

Malcolm watched the nurse intently, she was a ward sister, probably late forties early fifties, she had keen intelligent eyes and a stern expression; she was clearly nobody's fool. The nurse stared back blankly for a second and then smiled.
'We're expecting you? Yes, yes of course, you're here to see . . . ?'
'Mrs Watkins.'
'That's right yes, come with me.'
They followed her down a narrow corridor that smelled strongly of bleach, turned a corner, then another, finally entering a cramped corner room. The woman lay in the narrow hospital bed fast asleep, a drip was attached to one of her arms.
'You'll see that we're not disturbed.'
'Of course doctor, 'the nurse left closing the door behind her.
'We're not going to get anything out of her whilst she's . . .'Malcolm began.
'I'm not looking to get anything out of her, at least not in the sense that you mean.' The woman walked over to the drip and read the name on the bag then took hold of the woman's arm to examine the cannula. 'Come here make yourself useful, gel your hands first.'
Malcolm grabbed the cleaning gel from the tray beside the bed and did as he was told.
'Right hold her arm.'
'I assume you know what you're doing?'

She ignored him turned the clip to switch the drip off and gently pulled the cannula from the woman's arm then placed a small cotton swab over the puncture wound, 'Finger.'

Malcolm held the swab in place with a finger whilst she cut a length of surgical tape. She folded a quarter of an inch of the tape at either end back on itself, then gently but firmly taped the swab to Adele's arm. Malcolm watched her work, despite the difficulty she had with her one hand she worked quickly and expertly. Anyone watching would immediately assume that she was a professional nurse who'd been doing this for years.

Once done she pulled a chair up beside the bed and motioned Malcolm to do the same. She placed her good hand on the woman's forehead and turned to Malcolm. 'This will take a while.'

They sat in silence for fifteen minutes or so, until the woman's eyelids started to flicker.

'Adele my name is Joanne I'm here to explain to you what happened on the bus, I've come here to tell you what happened on the bus. I need you to open your eyes. I assure you that you are completely safe.' The woman's voice was like music, soothing, reassuring and completely trustworthy.' Adele's eyes flicked open.

'I want you to look into my eyes Adele, there we are now.'

The woman leaned over the patient, bringing her face closer

to her. 'Now you are completely safe, look at me Adele, look at my eyes and you can see that I'm telling you the truth. There is nothing that can harm you here.' She took Adele's hand. 'You believe me don't you?'

Adele nodded after a moment hesitantly at first but then more firmly.

'Now Adele let me tell you what happened.'

'I did see them, horrible, terrible, they were there,' Adele stammered.

'I know you did darling, I'm not here to argue just to explain. Now you live in Usk don't you?'

'Yes,' Adele managed her voice a little calmer but her eyes kept darting around the room.

'Now Adele I've already told you that you're safe, haven't I?'

'Y yes.'

'You can see that I'm not lying to you, can't you? Look at my eyes Adele.'

Adele did and this time she didn't look away.

'That's much better Adele, now keep looking at me and I'll explain. You live in Usk so you know about ROF Glascoed, the Royal Ordinance Factory at Glascoed?'

'Yes, up the road in little Mill.'

'Glascoed is an ammunition filling facility that works for the ministry of defence. They are experts in all types of weapons.

'Yes.'

'Adele the army recovered a weapon that had been obtained by a terror cell, the weapon was a powerful hallucinogen called ADT. The chemical is stored as a gas; anybody exposed to that Gas will see the most terrible, horrible things. The gas affects all of the senses, even the way that time passes. Monstrous things will move at terrible speeds and it will all be completely real. An army exposed to this gas cannot fight. The soldiers collapse in terror, that's what the gas was developed for, that's what it does. This gas is completely illegal Adele, when the army recovered it they sent it to Glascoed to be destroyed. They have a laboratory there that can do this but a canister was stolen, nothing sinister, a disgruntled former employee just wanted to make a point. He didn't even know what ADT was. He left the canister on a bus assuming that it would be found and his former section leader would get into a lot of trouble but there was an accident and the canister was ruptured.'

She repeated the story, using exactly the same words, three times. She spoke slowly and calmly but there was a real authority in her voice. She was completely believable to such an extent that Malcolm even started wondering about what had really happened. If he hadn't seen the film from the cctv on the bus . . .

Before long Adele was sat up in bed, angry now more than anything else. 'Why would they do such a thing, make people think they're losing their minds. It wasn't British gas was it?'

'No, my goodness me no, the British army sticks firmly at all times to the Geneva convention and the UN codes of conduct in warfare.' Malcolm replied automatically to Adele, drawing a sly grin from the other woman who was pressing the call button for the nurse.

'What about the chappie who left in on the bus, probably get off with a slapped wrist, Judges these days.' Adele grumbled.

'Oh far from it,' Malcolm lied expertly. 'He's already in custody and he won't be seeing the outside of a prison for a very long time.'

'What about the gas, could have gone anywhere?' Adele still wasn't happy.

'All the canisters have trackers put on them, as soon as it was outside of the base several specialised units were sent to recover it. They couldn't prevent the accident but they could neutralise the gas as soon as they arrived.' Malcolm continued effortlessly utilising years of experience in creating cover stories.

The sister they'd seen earlier entered the room and stared in disbelief at Adele who was wagging her finger angrily at Malcolm. 'I'm going to want compensation, I've missed 'Enders and Emmerdale and did anyone go to my house and feed Leroy? – I doubt it, soldiers running around, buses being gassed up. I don't know what the worlds coming to, I'm telling you now I'm going to want compensation, this wasn't what we fought a war for. Where there's a blame there's a claim. I've seen the adverts, I know how it works, I want compensation.' She said all of this without pausing for breath.

'Doctor Smith What? - How on earth . . .?' The astounded sister managed after a moment.

'Ah sister the woman replied, thrusting her damaged hand back into its pocket before the nurse saw it. 'Could you organise a light breakfast for . . .'

'I want full English!'

'And a cup of Tea.'

'Coffee, latte three sugars'

'For Adele please, thank you.' She swept out of the room causing Malcolm to scurry after her and leaving the sister lost for words. They reached the door with the numeric keypad. '1664' she told Malcolm who keyed in the number and opened the door.

'ADT?' He asked as they headed for the car park.

'Any damn thing,' she told him.

'Is it Joanne?'

'No.'

'Might I ask what it is?'

'It's not Joanne.'

They walked out of the building and both took a long breath of the cool bleach free air outside.
'Can I get you breakfast?'
'Someone of your acquaintance knows my name, she doesn't have your intellect, nor all the clues to my identity that you have but she's already worked it out. She's why I'm here!'

Midday Friday found the three of them bunched around Reds 'desk' in the library. Red had spent the morning on the internet and the boys met her with sandwiches for lunch.
'Say that again,' Steve said through a mouthful of cheese and pickle.'
'Malcolm's got somebody inside the school to keep an eye on us.' Red repeated as she removed the tomatoes from the beef and tomato sandwich's that the boys had brought her.
'What did I tell you? What did I say?' Ethnic exclaimed as he struggled with his sandwich wrapper.'
'Nothing mate,' Steve replied unimpressed taking some of the tomato pieces off red.
'Didn't mention anything,' Red added.
'Ok but I was thinking it and I told you when they bugged the car.'
'You told us after they told us if I remember right,' Red corrected.

'Ok but we're missing the point here, who it is'' Ethnic thought for a moment. 'I bet it's that new girl in the office,' he suggested struggling with the top of his coke bottle.
'She's blind how can she be keeping an eye on us.' Steve pointed out.
'That's just what they'd expect us to think.'
Red took the bottle off Ethnic, 'She partially sighted, she's a real sweetie her names Justine and it isn't her, it's the new supply teacher in Biology, Mr Franks.'
'How do you . . .?'
'That's what I've spent the morning doing, he came to us after working in Castleton right?'
'Yep.'
'Well there's 2 comps. In Castleton I've rung both of them this morning asking if Mr Franks had moved yet neither of them had heard of him.'
'Makes sense, he's in Biology and the running group.' Steve conceded.
'Yeah but even then he only sees us now and again, blimey do you think he's bugged here?' Ethnic asked looking under the desk.
'No it's a case of getting someone on site, rather than following us around. That way if anything kicks off here they can get involved or get help.'

The boys sat thoughtfully for a moment as Red examined Ethnic's coke bottle. 'Have you dropped this Ethnic?' she asked brandishing the bottle.

'No.'

'Have you been playing catch with this bottle of coke Steve?'

'No.'

'Or shaking it.'

'No.'

'Okay just checking,' Red easily twisted the cap off the bottle which promptly exploded and sent coke spraying over Ethnic and herself.'

'Mike had the bottle for a while mind.' Steve added helpfully.

'Oh way to go Steve thank you so much!' Red shrieked thumping him twice.

Any further violence was curtailed by the appearance of Maddy a second year who was holding an envelope in one hand and her mobile in another. 'Davros and the losers' she 'read' aloud from the envelope before dropping it into Red's lap.

'Goodness she can read.' Ethnic quipped.

'Least I can get coke from its bottle to my mouth without plastering everyone and everything with it.' The girl retorted slowly shaking her head as she left.

'She's got a point.' Steve observed.

'Guys this is it, the treasure hunt sanctions!' Red shouted.

Ethnic and Steve swung their chairs either side of Red who was frantically tearing open the envelope.

Jenifer, Jamel and Eli
You'll no doubt be aware that there have been calls made upon me by the school social committee to either ban the three of you or impose sanctions on you, following your previous four victories in the summer and Christmas treasure hunt events.
I have written to inform them that a ban would be unconstitutional and contrary to the philosophy of the school where we seek to encourage and reward excellence, not punish it.
However I do accept that the three of you do need some form of handicap in order to keep the event interesting and give everyone else a chance. I confess I did toy with the idea of splitting the three of you up and placing each of you with the three groups that failed to finish last year's event. This however seemed a trifle harsh so after some thought I think I've hit upon a more elegant solution.
As you are aware the event normally starts at lunchtime and the participants are on foot or in a wheelchair. As both Eli and Jamel are now loose on the highway I've decided to set another treasure hunt just for you three before the main event. This will start 9.30am sharp and you will need a car. Whichever of you is driving will go to the main office at

9.15am where Mrs Watkins will give you the envelope and £40 cash for fuel.
If you complete the first event before lunchtime you can start the second with everybody else, you can only start the second event however *after* you've completed the first. In other words if you are an hour late after the first you'll be starting the second an hour after everybody else.
Hope you are all well and working hard.

Harold Williams.

'Aw come on!' Ethnic protested.
'Could have been worse I suppose,' Steve grumbled.
'Forty quid's pretty much a whole tank, that's three hundred miles. He'll have us driving round the whole country.'
Ethnic wasn't impressed, 'And if he's setting clues for just us they're going to be a nightmare.'
Steve nodded solemnly
Red however was more optimistic, 'Guys it's an extra hunt, we'll have the whole day, this is great, what . . .'
'Don't say it Red.'
'Red no don't, don't say it.'
'What can possibly go wrong.'
'She said it!'

The Song of Tec

'In a castle of stones, a broken bell rings'
'Ready to fight come sisters with wings'
'With a mortal's help and a morning's light'
'The two sided sword ends the creatures of night.'
'But the fault is mine and there's nowhere to hide.'
'The children are lost, who'll stand at my side.'
'Who do I turn to, with what do I fight.'
'I must find soldiers who can tear down this night.'
'I'll go to that place where all hope's a lie'
'And find me an army that know not how to die.'
'But the children of shadow will never be found,
'Whilst the soldiers of silver sleep cold in the ground.
So I'll search long and hard through darkness and flood,
And I'll bring soldiers of glass and soldiers of blood.'

48520878R00143

Printed in Poland
by Amazon Fulfillment
Poland Sp. z o.o., Wrocław